**"This is Remy Beaumont, newest addition to our writing team—part intern, part advisor. He's got a** degree in magical monsters, so he's gonna help keep your backstories straight, as well as bring in different species of guest stars."

Ash managed enough courage to raise his gaze to Remy once again. He looked… God, better than he had months ago, which was terribly unfair. He had a longer hairstyle that better suited his face, and new glasses with large frames that made his eyes pop.

Remy waved and smiled at them. "Hello."

Ash wanted to lunge across the table and kiss him. He looked away, surprised by the fierceness of the desire. His heart pounded.

"Remy, meet the lovely and hilarious Jasmine, the charming and beautiful Michael, and our shy and sweet Ash."

"Nice to meet you," Remy said to Jasmine and Michael, then turned to Ash and tilted his head, asking permission.

"We've already met."

# WELCOME TO

## DREAMSPUN DESIRES

Dear Reader,

Love is the dream. It dazzles us, makes us stronger, and brings us to our knees. Dreamspun Desires tell stories of love featuring your favorite heartwarming heroes, captivating plots, and exotic locations. Stories that make your breath catch and your imagination soar.

In the pages of these wonderful love stories, readers can escape to a world where love conquers all, the tenderness of a first kiss sweeps you away, and your heart pounds at the sight of the one you love.

When you put it all together, you find romance in its truest form.

Love always finds a way.

*Elizabeth North*

Executive Director
Dreamspinner Press

# Morgan James

# LOVE CONVENTIONS

PUBLISHED BY

Published by
DREAMSPINNER PRESS

5032 Capital Circle SW, Suite 2, PMB# 279,
Tallahassee, FL 32305-7886 USA
www.dreamspinnerpress.com

Love Conventions
© 2019 Morgan James.
Editorial Development by Sue Brown-Moore.

Cover Art
© 2019 Alexandria Corza.
http://www.seeingstatic.com/
Cover content is for illustrative purposes only and any person depicted
on the cover is a model.

Paperback ISBN: 978-1-64108-103-0
Digital ISBN: 978-1-64080-728-0
Library of Congress Control Number: 2018966304
Paperback published May 2019
v. 1.0

Printed in the United States of America
∞
This paper meets the requirements of
ANSI/NISO Z39.48-1992 (Permanence of Paper).

**MORGAN JAMES** is a clueless (older) millennial, who's still trying to figure out what she'll be when she grows up but is enjoying the journey to get there. Now, with a couple of degrees, a few stints in Europe, and more than one false start to a career, she eagerly waits to see what's next. Morgan started writing fiction before she could spell and wrote her first (unpublished) novel in middle school. She hasn't stopped writing since. Geek, artist, and fangirl, Morgan tends to pass free hours with imaginary worlds and people on pages and screens—it's an addiction. As is her love of coffee and tea. She lives in Canada with her massive collection of unread books and acts the personal servant of too many four-legged creatures. Twitter: @MorganJames71

Facebook: www.facebook.com/morganjames007

For Ashlyn, without whose support, encouragement, and feedback this novel would never have existed, and who understands the love that fueled it. You are the best friend, co-author, and cheerleader anyone could ask for. Thank you.

# Part I
## Toronto

## Chapter One

**ASHLAND** Wells smiled as he thanked the trembling, eager fan one last time before she rushed away, and then he turned to the next person in line.

A woman approaching forty stood behind a kid maybe thirteen or fourteen. Ash felt his smile warm and held out his hand for the promo shot the kid had picked from the array on the table.

"Hello," Ash said. Not many wee ones came to his table—his biggest hit, *Restraint*, hadn't exactly been kid-friendly—but he tended to get more than a couple of smitten teens. "I'm Ash."

"I know," the boy breathed, staring at Ash with large dark eyes. Behind him, his mother pressed her lips together, hard.

Ash's smile widened. "Yeah, I guess you do." He glanced down at the Post-it stuck to the picture. "Declan, is it?" Declan nodded, his head wobbling alarmingly, like a bobblehead. "Well, nice to meet you, Declan." Ash smiled, and the kid looked like he might swoon.

Still smiling, Ash turned back to the picture. Declan had picked a promo shot from the final series of *Restraint*, in which Ash's character looked unusually confident and healthy. Ash scrawled *To Declan, "I'm one of the good guys." Ashland Wells* across the picture. On a whim, he added a heart.

He capped the Sharpie and looked up, ready to engage with the kid.

Declan stared at him. "You're my favorite," he blurted. "I love Zvi. He's the best." He blinked his calf eyes and turned bright red.

Ash smiled gently. The teens just might be his favorite fans, always so genuine and sweet. "Thank you. I'm happy to hear Zvi means so much to people." He slid the picture across the table. "I hope you're having fun this weekend."

Declan nodded again, and after he gushed some more and thanked Ash a couple of times, he floated away with the picture clasped to his chest. His mother mouthed a thank-you at Ash and then followed.

Whenever Ash grew weary at a con, a fan like Declan would show up and remind him why he did them. Plenty of actors never went or only attended San Diego when ordered to, but Ash felt he owed his fans something. Besides, their appreciation really was gratifying.

Three days of meet and greet wore him out, though.

"Do you think Zvi and Moira were soul mates?" sighed one woman dreamily. "The moment you came on the show, I knew you and Moira were meant to be."

"Well, attraction was the intent. They told me that before I got the part." He smiled at her and signed a picture of wolfy Zvi curled around his lover—a fan favorite.

As much as Ash loved Zvi, he discharged his guardianship duties of the character after the finale. He'd held his breath with every new script, worried that would be the week they ruined his character. But Zvi—and Ash—made it through six series with fairly consistent development, which ended with Zvi and Moira together. He needn't say more.

This fan didn't agree, apparently. "Do you think Zvi and Moira have kids?"

Ash blinked. "I don't think Zvi has ever thought about bairns. They lead a well-dangerous life." Her face fell. "But you know Zvi, whatever Moira wants, right?"

"Right!" she said and soon bounded away.

Sat on his right, Etta Hayes chewed her lips to hide her amusement, and Ash flicked her knee hard under cover of the table.

He got his first body-part request of the con about twenty minutes after that. Thank Rodenberry's ghost he was scheduled for a break right after.

Yawning over a tea, Ash wished they hadn't flown in so late the night before. He and Etta had taken an evening flight from Vancouver to Toronto. They still weren't late enough to avoid people waiting outside the hotel with their cameras. Ash in his old jeans, Henley, toque to hide the ginger, and shades was definitely on Twitter by now.

"Photo ops up next," Etta said. She sipped her lemon-ginger tea and scrolled through the schedule on her phone.

Ash hid a grimace. Given the choice, he'd decline to take pictures with fans, but every convention featured photo ops. Ash's un-Scottish personal bubble stretched about two meters wide. Sometimes he felt crippling jealousy of John Barrowman and his lack of shame.

The fans loved the ops, though. So every con, he put on his big-boy trousers, smiled like he meant it, and got his picture taken, over and over.

This photo shoot passed like the rest. Some fans wanted an arm around the shoulders, some to pose as werewolves. Some showed up in *Restraint* cosplay as Moira, Grif, Kliah, or even Zvi and wanted to pose in character. A few people surprised him—like the brick-house young man who asked to lift Ash off his feet. Ash eyed the lad, who obviously outweighed his own fifteen stone, and asked, "Can you do it without dropping me?" It turned out he could.

As much as Ash had a reputation for refusing to sign skin—his speech about body autonomy was well practiced—he had another for indulging pose suggestions. He imposed limits, of course—he turned down any request involving his ass—but for most, he was game.

The flash went off and Ash relaxed out of his Moira pose, the fan from her Zvi. He shook her hand, wished her well, then turned to greet the next person but found no one. He looked at Lisa, the photographer, who shrugged.

"According to my schedule, a Remy Beaumont should be here right now. Then you've got a twenty-minute break."

Ash cast about—as if this Remy might hide behind the tripod—but saw only Etta and Lisa in the wee curtained-off space. He shrugged and took a sip of his water. He felt a twinge of pity for the unknown fan. Cons tended to be strict about the photo ops—no rescheduling missed appointments.

Ash was screwing the cap back onto the bottle when he heard the first *sorry*.

A young Doctor, Ten, barreled into the booth. He stumbled to a halt. Panting, he waved his ticket and said, "Sorry! Sorry I'm late!" and then handed the paper to Lisa. He ran one long-fingered hand through messy black hair. He was appropriately skinny for his costume choice and wore a pair of black-plastic-framed glasses. His eyes were a bright, startling green—*Harry Potter eyes*—and his skin a light brown.

Lisa read the ticket. "Remy, you're lucky you got here when you did." She checked his name off on her list and waved him over. Ten—Remy—turned and beamed at Ash. Then he stepped forward and, in those six feet between them, tripped over... something. He fell to his knees, skidded the remaining few inches, and came to a stop at Ash's feet. Or rather, he stopped when his hands landed on Ash's thighs and his face near collided with his crotch.

Ash froze, staring down at the man who, for one agonizing second, pressed his forehead to Ash's belly, which had thankfully taken the brunt of the collision. Ash's ears burned. The thought of what Etta might say mortified him, and he hadn't been the one to trip.

Remy stayed down, his head bent and his shoulders quivering.

*Oh God, he's crying.* Ash hated when fans cried—though here was new motivation for why—and was ready to panic, when Remy threw his head back and... laughed.

And not an hysterical "if I don't laugh, I'll cry" sort, but full-on "life is hilarious" guffaws.

After a minute, he calmed enough to say, "Oh God. I thought being late would be the worst of it." He wiped tears from his cheeks. Collected, he stood and offered a hand. "I'm Remy and I'm so very sorry about the unintentional grope. Definitely didn't do it on purpose. I mean, you're cute and all, but I tend to ask permission first." He smiled.

On autopilot, because Maw taught him manners, Ash clasped his hand. How to take this man who could trip and land in such a compromising position but laugh about it so easily? Despite Ash's lack of body modesty—Zvi spent his first series nearly naked—he'd never mastered shaking off embarrassment.

"No hard feelings, I hope?" Remy asked, some of the levity slipping from his expression. "I mean, if you wanted to call security on me, I wouldn't blame you. Honestly I think I've burned up all my time on this. But, uh…." He stumbled to a stop, apparently out of things to say at last.

Years of training took over, and Ash's mouth said, "No, s'alright. Accidents happen, aye?"

"For sure." Remy looked at Lisa, eyes wide. "Do I still have time for a picture?"

Lisa nodded. "Barely." Ash caught her eye and tried to let her know he didn't mind losing a minute or two of his break. She nodded.

"Yay," Remy said quietly but enthusiastically. He gave Ash an expectant look.

"Right. What did, did you have in mind?" And now *Ash* sounded the starstruck one.

"Well," Remy said, drawing out the word, his smile growing brighter, "I read somewhere you're a *Doctor Who* fan."

Ash nodded. He used to watch it with his brother—his maw's VHSs in the nineties, and the reboot in the noughties.

"And I think your favorite companion was Donna?"

Ash nodded again. He never got used to strangers knowing so much about him. "Gingers gotta stick together."

Remy pulled a red wig out of his pocket. "Want to be my companion?"

Over the years, Ash had held plenty of props for these pictures, but never a wig.

He shrugged and took it, leaned forward, slipped it on, and then straightened and tried to tame the locks into some sense of order. Remy watched him, the picture of delight.

How did Ash's square jawline and stubble look framed by long strands?

Ash put his hands on his hips and said, in his best Donna voice, "Oy, Spaceman. We posing here, or what?"

Remy laughed. "Definitely. *Allons-y!*" He stepped up beside Ash and then seemed to falter. "How should…?"

"On the cover of the box set, she's behind him, aye?"

Remy's eyes widened. Hopefully the hair covered Ash's burning ears. At least he hadn't admitted how *often* he rewatched that series.

Remy positioned himself with one hand outstretched toward the camera to halt the oncoming danger, the other thrust to the side as if trying to keep Ash safe—or maybe from rushing forwards.

Ash crouched behind Remy, which wasn't impossible, given Remy was almost of a height, and leaned left to peer round his shoulder, doing his best to keep his chest or thighs from touching Remy. He placed his hands on Remy's arm and discovered a surprising bit of whipcord muscle under the suit.

*Focus.* What did Donna's expression look like? Knowing the character, concerned but curious probably.

The camera light flashed, and they were done.

Ash straightened and broke contact, though the heat lingered in his palms. Then he noticed Etta had moved nearer the camera and was holding up her phone. Ash arched a brow.

She shrugged and smiled sweetly. "Of course I'm taking a picture of you with the long locks. They suit you." Ash knew better than to disagree.

Remy bounced on the balls of his feet. "Nisha is gonna freak to see you in her Donna wig."

Ash gently extricated himself from it, well-careful now he knew it a loaner, and handed it over. "That was a good idea."

"Thanks! I was aiming for something different. You probably get lots of people asking you to be Zvi."

Ash nodded. "It's fun, though," he said, mindful that fans talked to each other.

"Sure, sure. This was awesome. I was going to get you to sign my copy of a script, but thought of this, and then couldn't make up my mind but…."

Ash glanced at the clock. His breaks acted as buffers to avoid lagging too far behind schedule and provided time for the loo. Ash didn't have to pee. "Script?"

"Yeah. A friend did some work on *Restraint* and had a copy of the script for 'Howling' and gave it to me as a gift. She knows me well."

Usually Ash followed the rules Etta laid down regarding not doing free pictures or autographs while at cons. But sometimes….

"I don't suppose you have it with you?"

Remy's eyes widened. "Yeah?"

"Pull it out." And Ash hoped no one else noticed the double entendre. He turned to Etta—who was

clearly trying not to laugh—and she handed over one
of the many Sharpies she kept in her purse. He always
forgot to carry them, despite both their efforts.

The script was from series four, the episode where
Zvi runs into his sister. It might be the episode Ash
was most proud of, given the emotional range and the
toll it had taken. Maybe that was why he offered a free
autograph.

He opened the protective cover, and bracing the
sixty-or-so pages against his right arm, he wrote *To
Remy* across the top over the title and, inspired, added *a
great companion*. He followed it with a Zvi line—*I've
got claws; what have you got?*—and signed it.

He handed it back to Remy, who vibrated with
excitement. "Oh man, this is too great. Thank you so much."

Ash wrinkled his nose. "No' a problem. Though
maybe don't tell too many folk about this. Not supposed
to sign stuff away from the table."

"Right, of course. Thanks again, so much. I'm a big
fan of where you took Zvi. I know, 'just an actor,' but
you had some influence, and he wasn't the throwaway
or the stereotype he could have been. So yeah. Thanks
for being awesome?"

Ash ducked his head and rubbed his nape, stupidly
shy under the praise. He'd heard this sort of thing from
fans before. "Thank *you*." He raised his gaze. "I wouldn't
be here without fan support." Zvi's role on the show had
grown and lasted thanks to viewer enthusiasm.

"I bet you say that to all the boys." Remy waved it
off, but he still smiled.

Instead of one of his stock answers, Ash opened
his mouth and said, "Only to the Tens."

Remy threw his head back and laughed with
delight.

Pleasure bubbled in Ash's stomach. He looked away and caught Etta's eye. She arched one naturally perfect eyebrow. Ash swallowed and turned back to Remy—*the fan*.

"Etta is giving me the 'time to hurry up' face." Ash was well-familiar with that look, even if she didn't currently wear it. He held out a hand. "Nice meeting you, Remy."

They shook goodbye, and then Remy collected his things and left with one last waggle of his fingers, an "Allons-y!" and a bounce in his step.

Etta tutted. "You need a bathroom break? As it is, you got like ten minutes before the next group of pictures."

Ash shook his head.

"All right. Remember, though, last chance for another hour."

"Thanks, but I'm alright," he said dryly, "and a big boy."

Etta rolled her eyes and muttered something that sounded suspiciously like "Doubt it."

AN hour later Etta led Ash toward the green room. Then, because Ash felt crowded, they went out a back door and wandered a ways from the building, out of sight of swarming attendees.

Etta broke the silence. "He was a cutie."

Ash didn't need to ask who.

"Should have gotten his number."

He glared at her.

"What? He totally wanted to give it. You could do much worse than a cutie who shares your passion for cheesy sci-fi."

"*You* watch that cheese with me," Ash grumbled, hoping to change the subject. She didn't often bring up such topics in public. Nervous, his hand rose to touch the coin hung between his pecs and behind his shirt. He glanced round, but no one was about.

Etta snorted. "Yes, because I've forgotten how to be discreet after all this time," she snapped.

Ash grunted softly but stopped looking about and settled his hand—an apology of sorts.

He'd got cast on *Restraint* at twenty-two, long before he'd figured himself out. By the time he realized he was gay, he'd already become famous in certain circles. He shuddered at the memory of what happened to queers who were found out in Hollywood. It was easier to hide.

"You know I only want you to be happy, right?" Etta sighed. "And like *I'm* going to ever tell you off for not dating."

She was a confirmed singleton, and only Ash ever heard her use words like *asexual* and *aromantic*.

He bumped their shoulders together, another apology. He'd be lost without her.

Etta rolled her eyes but pressed back. "All right, you *eejit*. Let's get back inside. We've got a schedule to keep."

## *Chapter Two*

**SATURDAY** and Sunday played out like Friday, with more photos and autographs. He took more funny shots—no one else asked him to be their companion, though he did arm wrestle a Klingon on the head of R2D2—signed more pictures of his face, and answered more questions. He rebuffed a couple of attempts to make him admit to dating the costar who played Zvi's love. Ash and Adele were no more involved than he was a werewolf. Ash never understood why anyone would dedicate a website to him and Adele. She thought it hilarious.

Sunday after lunch Ash had his panel—an interview onstage, in front of fans. At least he got to keep his personal bubble intact, but he wished Adele were there. She loved fielding the really embarrassing

questions. She'd once given a lengthy answer about
Moira and Zvi's sex life. Ash had insisted he'd never
given it much thought, other than that Zvi was "gun-
shy," much to Adele's laughing amusement.

Fortunately, that Sunday, most of the questions
were tame if somewhat repetitive. They asked about
his favorite episode and guest star, about his last guest
spot, asked if he could tell any stories about his time
on *Metropolis*, and what he'd do next. Ash knew those
answers.

Ash smiled and thanked a fan—a younger, chubbier
Moira—for her question, turned to the mic on the other
side of the auditorium, and saw a familiar coat.

"Hello," said Remy.

"Hi," Ash said, mouth dry. He swallowed and tried
to remember the script.

"I'm Remy," he said cheerily. "Good to see you
again."

"Hi, Remy. I'm Ash," he said by rote. He thought
about saying "I remember you," but a few hundred eyes
stilled his tongue. "What did you want to ask?" Ash put
down his mic, uncapped his water bottle, and took a sip.

"If you were stranded on a desert island, what three
things would you want with you?"

He wanted Ash's desert-island picks? After a pause
during which his mind scrambled, he brought the mic
up to ask, deadpan, "What kind of desert island are we
talking about? *Gilligan's*, *Castaway*, or *Lost*?"

The audience chuckled, but Remy's laugh rang
loudest through the sound system. "Well, I'm assuming
you won't have a coconut radio, a volleyball, or be in
purgatory...."

"Well, in that case." Ash scratched his nose,
thinking desperately. "I'd want some type of knife or

blade, for survival reasons. And, um, well, what about a coconut generator? Can I have one of those? Because I'd want an e-reader—I'd go crazy without a library for so long."

"Sure," Remy snickered. "Coconut generator just for you."

"Thanks. Uh, and one more?" He thought about it, then huffed a laugh. "What about people? Can I bring my bodyguard with me?"

"I'm not sure she'd be happy to be dragged along," Remy pointed out.

"She definitely would no'. But she'd increase my odds of survival by a whole lot." That got him some laughter, a few cheers. "She's tougher than I." Beat. "She's the one who disposes of spiders." The crowd loved that.

So did Remy, judging from the wide grin. "I guess you better take her with you, then."

"Thanks. Just, er, don't tell her that." Ash winked.

"Our secret." He mimed locking his lips. "Thanks." Then he ducked out of the way.

"Hi, Ash!" the next fan said, pulling Ash's attention away from Remy. "I wanted to ask about the most difficult scene you ever filmed. For *Restraint*."

Back on familiar territory. Ash stifled a sigh of relief.

The remainder of the panel was routine, like the rest of the day, at least until he and Etta were back in the hotel room by seven, with no plans to check out. Usually once a con ended, they caught a red-eye home, but he needn't hurry back to Vancouver this time. They had decided to stay on a couple of days to see some of the city. Ash had only ever been to Toronto for

promotional or convention work and usually saw nowt
but the airport and a hotel.

In the room at last, Ash peeled out of his skinny
jeans, put on joggers, grabbed his latest book, and
sprawled on the couch. His phone buzzed, cutting short
his sigh of relief.

*Nice look for you!* read his brother's text.

*??? What?*

The reply came quick. *Pic of you as Donna. Belter.*
It ended with a string of thumbs-up emojis.

Ash groaned. "Etta! Tell me you didn't send
Langston the picture?"

Etta slunk into the room, dressed in a hoodie and
yoga trousers. She settled onto the couch. "I love hotel
suites. Want room service?"

"Etta!" Ash glared. "Picture?"

She shrugged. "Sure. It was pretty cute. You in a
wig, snuggled up to your Doctor."

Ash continued to glare.

"I wasn't going to send it, but then after today, how
could I not?"

He grumbled. "What does *that* mean?"

"You blushed. The moment you saw him, you
turned red. You were like a ten-year-old with a crush.
It was adorable."

*Etta is a shit*, Ash typed to his brother, scowling at
his phone and avoiding her eyes.

*Aye but a useful one! Always sends the best
blackmail.* After a short pause, he added, *You shag him?*

Ash nearly yelped out loud. *No!!! He's a FAN!*

He blushed furiously. His brother should know him
well enough to know he would never. Had never ever,
point in fact. Not that Langston knew *those* details.

*Aye. Handsome fan dressed as your Doctor crush. Shoulda shagged him.*

*Bugger off. Go to bed.*

*Groan. Its not even 12 and am knackered. Weans are tiring.*

*Numpty. Go to sleep.*

Ash shoved his phone under his thigh and opened his book. Etta flicked on the TV and settled on ice hockey. Ash would never understand the Canadian obsession. Etta didn't even like most team sports, but she had a weird soft spot for this one.

Ash eyed her over the top of the page, then tried to concentrate on *Young Stalin*.

"So," she said over the sounds of skates on ice, "room service?"


**WHEN** it came to entertaining himself in a new city, Ash ran from tourist traps. He was willing to visit historical sites, but he wasn't keen on climbing the CN Tower, seeing a Jays' ball game, or stopping by the ROM. Well, he might go to the Royal Ontario Museum if it had a historical retrospective of television sci-fi.

Given it was a Monday morning in early June and halfway through the exhibition's run, Ash figured it'd be quiet. So he gave Etta a reprieve—she and museums didnae mix—and told her to take the day off. She smiled, a lioness circling an antelope, as she found a local kickboxing gym and booked time at a spa.

By ten, Ash, wearing his incognito toque once again, had his museum ticket and was headed through the doors.

The exhibit was all he'd hoped for: a chronological display of sci-fi shows, from early cinema serials to the present day, which also focused on analyzing popular themes and the various philosophical discussions the genre had weighed in on over time. In other words, geek heaven.

He was stood in front of the *Star Trek*'s INFLUENCES ON TV AND SOCIETY display when a newly familiar voice said, "I do love this part. It's important to give Spock his dues."

Ash turned. Beside him, Remy had fixed his eyes on the display. Gone was the *Doctor Who*–chic. Today he wore skinny jeans, a thin long-sleeve tee with the arms pushed up, and a bright cotton scarf.

He turned to Ash, grinning. Then his eyes widened, and he inhaled sharply. Guess he hadn't realized who he spoke to. But he rallied quickly and said smoothly, "I've been here before, obviously. You enjoying it?"

Ash swallowed hard. That smile disarmed. "Aye." He cleared his throat. "I've been enjoying myself. It's good."

Remy nodded too and took a half step in reverse. "Well. I'll let you get on with it," he said politely. He kept backing away, probably figured a fan would be unwelcome. He probably thought Ash didn't remember him.

"I thought," Ash blurted and Remy paused, "I saw something about *Doctor Who* this way." He waved a hand. "It's my favorite." Remy nodded. Ash took a fortifying breath. "And I'm guessing yours too. Spaceman, yeah?"

Remy's smile turned blinding. "You remember."

Ash blushed. "Your entrance was very memorable."

Remy laughed and placed a hand over his eyes with a dramatic flourish. "God." He chuckled and dropped the hand. "I really am sorry about that. Have I mentioned?"

"Aye. I ken it wisnae on purpose." Ash gave an awkward shrug.

"Good. I would like you to also know that I'm not a crazy stalker. I didn't follow you here. Honest. I just like the exhibit. The con made me want to see it again."

Logical. Ash often wanted to laze about with a sci-fi show the day after a con, and not only because they wiped him out.

"Anyway. You definitely have to see the *Who* display. Over fifty years of stuff—oh and the companions thing." Remy ushered him toward the relevant corner. Ash moved without thinking. It wasn't until they were reading about the cultural influences of British sci-fi that Ash realized Remy had invited himself along on his tour.

"Favorite Doctor?" Remy asked.

"My brother is a huge Tom Baker fan." Ash shrugged. *Ten.* "But all the new Doctors have been good. You?"

"Ten, as you might have guessed." Remy flashed a cheeky smile. "Doesn't help that I had a massive crush on him at sixteen."

Ash barked a surprised awkward laugh. Remy looked calm and unbothered despite having come out to a *stranger*. Who did that? Ash couldn't keep standing there like a dunderheid, staring. "N-no, I guess it wouldn't," he finally stuttered.

Remy winked and then pointed to a picture and started monologuing, but Ash couldn't focus on his words. He was too busy watching and wondering. Remy was confident and bubbly, his hands waving about with animation. Not hesitant or worried.

"Oh, have you seen the gender and sexuality section yet?" Remy's eyes danced. Ash shook his head. "You have to see it." He grabbed Ash's wrist and pulled him from *Doctor Who* and round the corner.

Ash followed blindly. His heart thumped. Remy's hand was warm and strong. His long fingers curled all the way round his wrist.

"It's awesome. It plots the changes in depictions of both. There's even a blurb about kink positivity, which really, there are whole sections of the internet geared towards sci-fi kink. Pon farr anyone?"

Ash snorted. He opened his mouth—to say what, he didn't know—but Remy pulled him into a new room, distracting him. Like the others, this room housed panels with text and pictures, display cases, and monitors for film clips.

The only way to do museums was to start at the beginning, so Ash turned left. Remy bounded after him.

"What are you so excited about?" Ash narrowed his eyes.

Remy hummed. "You'll see."

Like the other rooms, this one displayed chronologically. One of the first pieces was, of course, all about *Star Trek*.

"The future"—Ash waved at the pictures—"where racism doesnae exist, but sexism does."

"Yeah." Remy smiled crookedly. "Nisha, my BFF, hates it for that. She rants at it all the time."

They moved on, and Remy kept talking. He chatted throughout the *X-Files* and *Buffy* displays but went suspiciously quiet when Ash moved along.

Then he saw it: Restraint—Gender, Sex, Moira Ravenscraft, and Zvi Grey. Ash stared at the picture of himself dressed as a werewolf slave. In it, his hands were bound and he wore the collar Ash had developed a love-hate relationship with. It was a great tool to tap into Zvi's character but was also hot and itchy. The picture wasn't terribly revealing in terms of skin, but

Zvi wore an injured, vulnerable expression. Ash felt raw and uncomfortable. He turned away.

The panels talked about several aspects of the show, including Adele's heroine—three-dimensional and all woman—and Kliah's portrayal of an incubus, but at the end it talked about Zvi—former sex slave and graysexual. Ash always liked that Zvi wasn't a perpetually horny male cliché, but it was bizarre to see it written out in a museum exhibit, to see it mention the episode where Zvi struggled to figure out what it meant to be male and uninterested in sex. Ash had been thrilled when he read that script.

"I'm pretty proud of that episode. A few people griped, but… I thought we did good."

"You did," Remy agreed. "From what I saw, the complainers either thought asexuals were a myth or they wanted Zvi to stay asexual."

"Yeah." Some argued the episode made asexuality look like a thing needing to be cured. Ash wondered if they heard any of the conversation Zvi had with a young asexual man, which gave Zvi peace and allowed him to take the time to settle in his skin before he worried about relationships.

"Which," Remy said, "ignores the point of the conversation—that any sexuality is valid. Also, Zvi is all about recovery, regaining a sense of self after loss and moving on."

Ash blinked. That was what he always wanted to say with the character and why he thought him inspiring. Over six series, Zvi grew from broken slave into independent man.

Ash cleared his throat. "Pretty much what I always thought. Learning to want again wasn't a bad thing."

"Yeah," Remy murmured and nodded.

They fell silent.

Ash looked at the picture of Zvi and his asexual friend, Basil, who'd made several repeat appearances. Zvi looked so lost but so hopeful that Ash had to turn away.

"Damn. I thought showing you this would be a kick. Sorry, I didn't—"

Ash waved a hand. "It's fine. Good. Just odd to, to see myself like tha' when I know it's no' me."

Remy made an adorable face. "Well, I'm a dumbass. Let's get out of here. We'll go look at the picture room."

"Picture room?"

"Yup." He popped the *p* obnoxiously.

The picture room turned out to be an open space with a green screen that faced a large TV mounted under a camera.

"Now you too can be part of a sci-fi show or movie. Pick a scene, make a pose, and snap a pic," Remy said in a bad movie-guy voice and with a wave of his hand.

Ten-year-old Ash would have lost his mind. Twenty-eight-year-old Ash cleared his throat and asked, "How does it work?"

A second monitor, with step-by-step instructions, hung next to the first: pick a franchise, a background, and picture or film.

"Which format?" Remy asked.

Improv was never Ash's strength, so probably no films. And he kind of wanted a picture to keep.

Remy must have noticed his hesitation, because he hurried to say, "You can keep any photos. I've done this before, I don't need 'em."

Huh. For once, the potential for fan-leaked photos hadn't occurred to Ash.

He shook his head to clear the thoughts. "Right. Photo's good."

For some reason beyond comprehension, he suspected Remy would keep this experience between them. Which was definitely idiotic.

"Awesome." Remy clicked the camera icon. "Now we take our places and pose when it tells us to."

The large flat-screen showed a video feed of them on the *Falcon*.

"I get to be Harrison Ford." Remy grinned, winked, and struck a Han Solo pose, hands together, holding an imaginary gun. "Wanna be my Leia?" He batted his eyelashes.

Caught off guard, Ash clumsily tried to come up with a suitably Leia-like pose.

A countdown started on the TV—three… two… one.

A shutter snapped, and after a moment, the picture appeared. In it, Ash stood stiffly and his hands hung awkwardly at his sides.

*Save or try again?* the screen prompted.

"Aren't you supposed to be an actor?" Remy laughed. "Come on, thespian boy, *act*."

Ash wrinkled his nose. He hated improv—he thought too much and acted too little.

"Come on. You *are* Leia Organa. Feel the emotion," Remy said dramatically and gripped Ash's shoulders in a parody of a pep talk. A smile tugged at Ash's lips. "Feel the angst. Stuck doing all the work like a badass while your brother gets all the credit."

"Ouch." Ash shook himself. "Right. Princess, general, badass." He clasped his hands together as though psyching himself up. It was *mostly* for show.

He grabbed his own imaginary gun.

The second picture was better. Ash didn't really look like Leia—together they looked like two-thirds

of Charlie's Angels—but at least he didn't look like a
cardboard cutout with a stick up his ass.

The screen asked if Ash wanted to email it to
himself. Remy stepped away. Ash sent it and then was
asked if the museum could save and use the photo for
publication. He stabbed hard at the No button, even if
he felt a slight pang of disappointment over deleting
the original.

Remy dragged him into the food room.

"Food room?"

"Yeah, meals in pill forms. You know"—he affected
a deeper, voice-over tone—"fooood of the future."

Ash smiled. "Sounds… unappetizing."

"No way," Remy said with enthusiasm. "Well,
meal pills do. But they don't have those to eat. It's also
a café. It has ice-cream dots, Ash, ice-cream dots. Who
can resist them?" Remy bounced as he led Ash to the
coveted ice cream.

"Are you secretly five?"

"Ha! You figured me out." His eyes danced, and he
caught Ash in his gaze until he looked away.

The food room turned out pretty much as
advertised, but Remy's enthusiasm entertained when
the room didn't. It also distracted—Remy moaned
obnoxiously as he snacked.

That Ash found himself flattered by Remy's
somewhat reluctant offer to share was probably a sign of
madness. Remy didn't strike him as someone who often
handed over food unasked. Ash only took two dots.

They left the food exhibit and were passing the
room on gender and sexuality when a male voice said,
"I know. He's so hot."

"Uh-huh," agreed a female one. "I can't decide if
I'd rather fuck Zvi or Wells."

Ash froze. He was aware people talked about him that way, objectified him and told their friends fantasies about him. Hell, it wasn't like he'd never done it about others. But knowing and hearing were very different things.

"Wells, obviously," said the masculine voice. "I like the shy ones. They're always the freakiest." He laughed.

Ash burned. He couldn't bring himself to look at Remy.

"I know you do," said the woman. They were getting closer.

*Buggering fuck.* Ash did *not* want to run into fans this way.

Remy curled his hand around Ash's and pulled him away from the voices. Then he opened a door, pushed Ash inside, and followed after. He shut them into the janitor's closet.

Ash wanted to face-palm. He was hiding from his fans, in a closet. The irony was killing him.

Remy snorted. "I never thought I'd find myself *in* the closet," he muttered.

They stood close together. The bursting shelves and supplies on the floor left little room to maneuver. Remy was thin, and though he was muscular, some of his angles jutted into Ash—an elbow, a knee. Ash knew people admired his body, especially when he had the extra twenty pounds of muscles for playing Zvi, but he had always preferred less bulk in other men.

Not that he'd ever done anything to pursue it.

They stood in silence. Remy's hot breath gusted across Ash's cheek. Over the sound of their soft breathing and his thumping heart, Ash heard the fans laughing heartily, growing louder and then fainter again.

Ash fidgeted, unused to standing so close to a fan outside of cons. He had never been much of the actor stereotype—short on personal space and overly tactile. Remy apparently didn't have the same problem.

He placed a hand on Ash's elbow—for balance?— and asked in a hushed tone that sent shivers down Ash's spine, "Okay?"

"Yeah," Ash breathed, matching him for volume.

They stayed silent for a minute.

"I think they're gone," Remy whispered. "Should we brave it?"

Ash hesitated a couple of extra beats. He could live through another few claustrophobic seconds if it meant avoiding tweets about him hiding in museum closets with strange men.

He touched his hidden coin pendant and hoped they weren't caught.

"Think we'll be safe?"

"I don't know," Ash admitted.

Remy cracked the door, pressed his cheek to it, and peered out. "I think the coast is clear. No more scary fans," Remy whispered conspiratorially. He grinned. "Shall we make a break for it?"

Ash nodded. "Aye." They exited the closet, aiming for casual. Or Ash suspected Remy was also attempting to look cool, to not draw attention to himself. Ash hoped *he* wasn't failing quite so badly.

They snuck out of the exhibit and through the museum.

Ash stuffed his hands into his pockets when they got outside. "Where to now?" he asked impulsively.

Remy's eyes widened.

Oh. Stupid to assume he wanted to hang out. He probably already had plans—

A smile spread across Remy's face. "I know the perfect place." He ushered Ash away from the building and led him to a hole-in-the-wall which apparently sold "the best doughnuts ever."

Remy ordered half a dozen. Ash arched an eyebrow but didn't protest.

They weren't exactly in his approved diet— somewhere, the *Restraint* trainer probably recoiled in horror, not knowing why—but fuck it. He wasn't filming anything, so no one would fuss if he ate some carb bombs.

Remy tugged Ash to the back corner of the shop. They weren't exactly sheltered, but it wasn't a conspicuous spot.

Remy pulled out a plastic knife and waved it in the air before he quickly cut the Earl-Grey-and-lemon doughnut into quarters.

"Right. Pick your poison," he said cheerfully.

Ash reached out slowly and picked one up. He was skeptical, but he did like Earl Grey.

"Wow," he said around his mouthful.

Remy popped one of the quarters into his smiling mouth. "I know, right? Everything they make is so good. They had a walnut, thyme, and maple flavor last year."

Ash couldn't help it, he wrinkled his nose.

Remy chuckled. "I know. But they were so good. As amazing as all the other ones. Sadly, they rotate all but their most popular flavors, so they no longer make it."

"That's too bad." Ash tried not to eye the other half of the Earl Grey and lemon too covetously.

Remy pushed the plate closer. "Go on."

Ash took a piece and ate it. Remy ate the other one, then cut up the blueberries and cream, which was equally delicious. They followed it with a chocolate and sea salt, a rosemary and orange with honey glaze, a peanut butter and banana, and a key lime pie. Ash only mildly regretted eating six half doughnuts in one sitting.

"So, favorite one?"

"They're all so good," Ash said. "But I think I like the Earl Grey one best."

Remy shook his head good-naturedly. "I love the chocolate one, but I'm gonna go with chocolate every time." He shrugged. "I might have a problem."

"A chocolate problem? Because you always have to side with it, never against it?"

"Something like that. It has a terrible hold on me."

Ash licked his lips and tasted a hint of honey. He smiled. "These were definitely a good idea. Though you probably delayed my dinner by an hour. And I definitely need to check out a gym tomorrow."

Remy groaned. "I'm not sure I've ever been in a gym."

Ash raised his eyebrows, unconvinced, remembering Remy's slim but muscled body pressed to his own. Ash swallowed.

"No really. These bad boys"—he lifted an arm to flex a bicep—"come from dog-walking and hockey."

"You play hockey?" Ash asked, surprised. Ash thought hockey players were... bigger.

Remy snorted. "You're so Scottish. Yes, I play hockey. Despite being a geeky beanpole, I'm still *Canadian*. Mom taught me on our backyard rink. I've played my whole life. But my NHL dreams didn't last past age seven."

"You were only seven when you decided you couldn't go pro?"

"I don't have the passion or talent for it." Remy smiled. "Also it coincided with my phase of wanting to be a chocolate pirate."

Ash barked a surprised laugh. "What?"

"I told you I had a chocolate problem," Remy said, nonchalant.

"You wanted to go into a life of high-seas chocolate crime?"

"It seemed like a good idea at the time. I'd get to sail, live with my buddies, eat chocolate, and sing a lot."

"Sing?"

Remy grinned. "I might have had a *Muppet Treasure Island* phase too. It led to some misconceptions."

Ash laughed, charmed by the image of Remy at seven, running about in costume, convinced pirates lived in musicals. "So you like to sing?"

"Sure. Who doesn't? I'm terrible, but whatever." He cocked his head. "You?"

"Oh. Well. Not really." Ash wasn't fond of singing with an audience. He hummed in the shower when he was alone in the flat, but he hadn't sung near others since primary school.

"That's too bad." Remy cast about. "I guess it's too crowded around here to bust into a musical number." He sighed dramatically.

Ash appreciated the restraint. The less attention attracted, the better.

"Anyway. You ready to blow this pop stand?"

Ash stared. "Pop stand? Are you ninety?"

"Nope, but I do love a good dad joke."

They both stood and gathered their rubbish. As they walked out, Ash tossed it into the bin, and Remy said, "Nice shot. Lucky for you, otherwise I'd trash-talk."

Ash groaned. "Pathetic."

"I suppose you could do better?"

"Maybe. But I'm rubbish at serving up puns to order."

Remy laughed. "Master." He gave a sweeping mocking bow.

Ash wrinkled his nose and smiled. "So. Where…?"

Remy tapped his chin. "Hmm. Oh! There's a place only a couple blocks away." He waved up the pavement, and they headed north… or west?

At the next intersection, they turned right. Ash stuffed his hands into his pockets and enjoyed the silence.

He never needed to fill the quiet, but people often wanted him to talk and share. It felt *good* to be with someone who seemed as content to pass moments unmarked.

"Hmm. I shared one of my childhood dreams…," Remy said. Well. *Nearly* content.

"I don't think chocolate pirate—"

"I was very serious about it. I even had a hat and everything. Anyway, I think it only fair you tell me one of yours."

Ash had several secret dreams as a kid. Maw once told him he'd wanted to be a dinosaur at four, and by eight he'd moved on to astronaut.

He didn't mention that.

"I was obsessed with Superman when I was five. I had several tapes with cartoons. I had a costume my maw made for me, and I wore it almost every day for half a year. Told everyone I was gonna be him."

"Really?" Remy's eyes danced.

"Yeah." Ash cleared his throat. "I've never told anyone that."

They stopped at a crosswalk. Remy's eyes were narrowed, considering. He licked his lips and hummed in understanding.

Ash tapped his pendant. "Everyone wants cute stories from your past. My brother wilnae talk, and I try not to say much about my life. I don't see the point really." Ash bit his lip and looked away. The light changed and he stepped off the curb.

"Well, no one will hear the story from me. How else could I lord it over you?"

Ash looked over as they reached the other side of the street, and Remy winked.

The tension eased from Ash's shoulders. He didn't know why it was so easy to believe Remy, but it was.

## Chapter Three

**AS** they continued on, Remy filled the time with idle chatter about the streets and the sites they passed.

A few blocks from the bakery, Remy guided him to a shop with a busy front window, jammed with odds and ends, mostly clothes and accessories—an old lace dress, a stylish button-down matched with trousers, several pairs of shoes, some gloves, a fedora, and a cowboy hat.

Unconvinced, Ash obeyed Remy's flourishing wave and entered before him.

Vintage clothing—some more gently used than others—filled every nook and cranny. Rows of hangers hung over more racks, and shelves loomed over them. Hats clung to any spare inch, and boxes of gloves, wallets, scarves, and bags were crammed wherever possible. Thankfully the space was clean and organized—to some degree.

The shop begged to be browsed and invited curiosity.

Remy grinned and wound his way between the tightly packed rows. He picked up a hat that looked like felt and had a round top and a large floppy brim which drooped when he put it on.

He struck a pose, hands on hips. "How do I look?"

"Like an eejit?"

"Oh good. For a second there, I thought I'd failed." He took the hat off, put it back, then moved on. Ash followed, glancing round, eyeing the wares.

"Ooh." Remy reached into the racks and pulled out a jacket which probably hadn't been worn since 1987.

"What is that?"

"Glorious," Remy breathed emphatically.

"*That* is not glorious. That is…." Ash flicked one shoulder. "It has shoulder pads."

"So?"

"And what do you even call that color? Bogey?"

"Hmm, neon yellow-green?"

"That's not a name. It's a description."

"Hey, yellow-green is an acceptable name for a color."

Ash snorted. "Yes. I'm sure all the great artists use it."

Remy held the coat up and gave it a look. "To be honest, I'm not sure any artist paints with this color."

"I hope not." Ash shuddered. "Not if they want to sell anything."

Remy put it back and flicked through the hangers next to it. Ash's gaze was caught by a collection of gloves on the opposite wall. They weren't made for cold weather, but fashion. He especially liked a pair of lady's white evening gloves like he hadn't seen since his appearance on a period drama. Ash reached out and touched. They were soft, and when he flipped them over, he saw fine needlework, an intricate pattern winding from cuff to fingers. Beautiful.

"Ooh, pretty," Remy enthused from over his shoulder.

"Yeah. Old-fashioned."

Remy cocked his head. "I wonder how old they are. They look ooold."

Ash snorted. "Yeah. Makes me think of my time on *Highclere House*."

Remy laughed. "Oh man. You didn't get to wear gloves like these, though." He tilted his head to the side. "That would have been a very different and interesting story for the footman if you had."

The corners of Ash's mouth quirked, but he kept a straight face. "Very different. Not sure the grans of England would have been ready for that."

"I think you're underestimating grans," Remy said with an arched brow. He took a step back and made a production of giving Ash a once-over. "I think you'd rock a turn-of-the-century corset and skirt. Very you. And you have the waistline for it."

Giving in, Ash dropped the straight face and chuckled. He shook his head. "You know, my gran loves that show, was thrilled when I was on it. She was so proud. Only four episodes, but she brags."

"What, and not about Zvi?" They drifted farther into the store.

"Nah. She's veray proud of me for being 'so famous,' but she's never seen my 'beasties magic show.'" He naturally slipped into her brogue as he quoted her.

"She doesn't really—"

"She does. Pats my cheek and everything when she says it."

"Your grandmother sounds amazing," Remy sighed. "Mine would not brag if I was working on a sci-fi show. Mostly because she only watches CBC and the local Quebecois public access." He wrinkled his nose. "Not that I see her much. She's near Quebec City, and Mom was always too busy to visit when I was a kid, and now... well, I can't afford the trip."

"I'm sorry," Ash said softly. "Distance from family isn't fun."

"Thanks." Remy gave a small smile. "Oh *sweet*." Remy picked up a top hat and placed it on his head. "What do you think?"

"Ridiculous." And handsome. "It's too big for you. Good thing your ears catch it, otherwise it would fall over your eyes." Ash nearly cringed.

Remy squawked. "My ears aren't big."

"They really are," Ash said apologetically. Why was he still talking? "Sorry." The brim forced Remy's ears to curve downward in a stupidly charming way.

Remy huffed and adjusted the hat. "Well. I guess I won't be going to you for any more fashion advice." He didn't look angry, though.

Ash put his hands in his pockets and tilted his head. "I guess I shouldn't tell you, then, that you need a walking stick to complete the look?"

"Ooh, a cane." Remy clapped his hands and looked around, apparently not holding a grudge.

Ash nearly sighed in relief. *Not offended.*

"Do you think they have one in here somewhere?"

Ash arched a brow. "Probably. But... you're not actually going to buy that thing, are you?"

Remy turned back to him. "What? No. I wish." He pulled the top hat off and flipped it over. "I proba— yeesh." He put it back with exaggerated care.

Ash picked up the hat by the brim to get a look at the price tag. He whistled. Even he'd balk at dropping $200 on a hat, and he was comfortable thanks to *Restraint* and to his portion of his dad's life insurance and settlement. "Yeah. No."

"Right? Definitely not at that price. I'm just a poor grad student."

They moved on, leaving too-expensive headgear behind. "What—" Ash licked his lips. "—are you studying?"

"Hmm? Myths and legends."

Ash blinked. "You can get a degree in that?"

"Oh, sure. You can get a master's in anything really."

Ash snorted. "So, what do you do with a degree in myths and legends?"

"If I'm lucky, I'll write a couple of best sellers and never have to work again. Worked for JK Rowling."

Ash wrinkled his nose. "She doesn't have a degree i—"

"So it's in classics. To-mato, to-mahto." Remy waffled a hand back and forth.

"Equally useless?"

Remy tossed his head back and laughed. His throat looked so long and his shoulders so broad as they shook. Ash blinked and turned away for a moment.

"Sorry." He straightened. "That was probably too loud." He smiled sheepishly. "I might have some tension regarding what the fuck I'm going to do when I graduate."

Ash shrugged and picked up an old knitted hat. He studied the Fair Isle pattern. "No worries. I, uh, had a few moments myself after drama school." He glanced Remy's way. Or this morning when he considered his lack of a gig.

"Oh, shut up. Like you didn't go to the Royal Academy and get the best pedigree an actor can get. Alan Rickman went there."

Ash's face heated. "And a lot of people you've never even heard of."

Remy snorted. "As if that would happen to you. You're too talented." He wasn't the first person to compliment Ash's acting, but his tone was so sincere and vehement Ash believed it.

"Thank you," he said softly.

Remy waved him off. "I tells it likes I sees it."

"But, uh, it takes a lot of luck, not just talent."

"Maybe," Remy said, but he didn't sound very convinced.

They continued through the aisles in an easy quiet. At the back of the store, they found an old table covered with and surrounded by baskets filled with small doodahs. Remy leaned forward to look at the basket of scarves and mufflers under the table, and Ash inspected the contents on top. There was a smaller box with ornamental pieces—a fascinator, a tiepin, a cuff link, and a large circular item.

Ash picked it up. It was a ring, only a few inches across, off-white, and made from a natural material. Ash wrinkled his nose. Ivory, maybe? It was finely decorated. Patterns curved around the surface on one side, and on the other were several Chinese characters.

He wondered what it was for. Scarves, maybe? Might work to hold the ends together. Ash flipped it back over, traced the delicate patterns with his fingertips. It was smooth as silk and expertly made. He turned it a few times but found no further inspiration as to its purpose.

A choked noise interrupted his thoughts. Ash looked over. Remy stared at the ring in his hands. "Wha-what's that?"

Ash shrugged. "Dunno."

"Oh," Remy squeaked and then cleared his throat. "Once upon a time, I took a History of Sex course, which was mostly a history of things humans make because of it—art, writing, sex toys." He looked at the object again.

Ash looked at him blankly. Then down at the... thing. "What, this?"

"I'm pretty sure." Remy's lips quivered.

"But it's a ring."

Remy pressed his lips together, then unclenched to say, "Yeah. But I'm pretty sure it's an old Chinese cock ring."

Ash's heart stuttered and nearly stopped when Remy said "cock."

Wait. What?

Ash looked down and noted the width of the opening. It would be appropriately sized to fit *some*—

Ash carefully but quickly dropped the ring back onto the table, and Remy gave in to his laughter.

Ash's face burned. *Oh God.* Why did a clothing store have antique sex toys? Why did Ash have to pick it up? Or Remy recognize it? Buggering fuck!

"You should—" Giggle. "Oh man, your face," Remy gasped.

Ash continued to burn. Why didn't floors ever open up and swallow people?

"I don't think I've ever seen a man so insulted by a cock ring, and that includes my ex with the hair trigger."

Ash's mouth dropped open. He stared.

Remy laughed and covered his face with his hands. "Sorry. Just, the look on your face."

Recovering somewhat, Ash glared. "Dick."

Remy's eyes widened. He giggled again, pressing one hand to his mouth to stifle the noise. Appalled at his accidental wordplay, Ash scowled harder, which only made Remy's laughter worse. His eyes, visible over his hands, were tearing. He looked ridiculous. Ash's lips twitched, and suddenly he too was laughing—big gasping laughter that shook his shoulders and shut his eyes. For a moment, he could hardly breathe as the hysterics took over.

Lightness filled Ash's almost-aching belly. It had been too long since he'd laughed like this—with unrestrained childlike abandon. He even forgot to worry about anyone watching.

"Oh God." Remy wiped his flushed cheeks, and his eyes sparkled.

Ash wrinkled his nose and rubbed his nape, once again aware of his surroundings.

"So…." Remy smiled at him. "You gonna buy it?"

"What? No!"

"Too bad." Remy picked it up and looked at the price tag. "Hmm, wonder if my old prof would want it."

Ash's eyes nearly bugged out of his head.

Remy snorted. "As a lecture aid, not to use, you dork." He looked back at the ring. "Fuck it. They want five dollars. Totally worth that." He slipped it around his long forefinger and gave it a spin.

Jesus. Who was this man?

"Ooh, spats." Remy picked up the black-and-white leather shoes and admired them from all angles. "Darn. Wrong size. Check out the wing tips, though."

Ash did and wondered if he should mention he owned a similar pair. They'd been given to him by a stylist before a charity event. He never liked wearing them; his feet looked huge. Give him a pair of Chucks or Blundstones any day.

"Right." Remy sighed and put the shoes back. "Maybe it's time to head out?"

He bought his cock ring and made light conversation with the clerk—"Yes, it is very pretty. Very detailed. Obviously ornamental, yeah."—and then they made a dash for the door. They held out until they were stood on the pavement and then gave in to the laughter again as they stumbled away and out of view.

They were still chuckling when they found a store where Ash could buy some souvenirs for his brother and his family.

Remy cast him dubious and judgmental looks as Ash made his choices.

"Really?" he asked when Ash picked up a mug with a picture of a beaver, and the captioni read "I don't give a dam before coffee."

Ash smirked. "Really. It's for Etta."

Remy laughed. "Far be it from me to argue, but sounds like a dangerous prospect."

"This?" Ash waggled the mug. "Nah, she'll love it. Not that she's not dangerous, mind. She's tossed me onto the ground on more than one occasion for being a bawheid."

"Now that," Remy laughed, "is something I'd love to see."

Ash winked and headed for the checkout.

"But," Remy said, as they left the store, "bawheid?"

Ash wondered if he should admit to the Scottish love of balls-based insults. Maybe not. "Bawheid's an eejit."

They ambled along aimlessly, and Remy swung his small bag with his antique cock ring back and forth. He did it distractedly, unconsciously, like a kid; it made Ash grin.

When it grew closer to tea, Remy pulled him into a restaurant with "the best wings, dude."

They settled at a table in the back corner. Ash placed his gifts at his feet. "Right." He eyed his menu. "What's good?"

"The wings." Remy shifted happily, apparently eager, and Ash lifted his eyebrows. "Of any flavor. They've got great spicy options, including a five-alarm one, if superspice is your thing. But the barbecue and honey garlic are amazeballs too, if you like something milder."

"Sounds good."

Twenty minutes later, Ash reassessed. Wings were a terrible idea. Despite their deliciousness, they had one major drawback. Remy wrapped pink lips around his left thumb and sucked it clean of sauce. It hypnotized. It was disgusting, of course, but Ash couldn't turn away, even as it made his stomach flip and fill with butterflies and his skin tingle with heat. Apparently, quiet, discreet eating wasn't something Remy did.

"You enjoying your wings?"

"Huh?" Ash blinked and refocused. Remy's green eyes danced, and they seemed to sparkle, even in the dim light. Ash hadn't known anyone actually had eyes that color. No one in his family had anything but muddy brown.

"The wings." Remy's lips quirked.

Ash coughed. "Oh, yeah. Veray tasty." He picked up a wing and waved it in demonstration. Then he took a bite.

*Shite! Fucking buggering bloody hell!* He'd grabbed one of the superspice ones. Blinking rapidly, he tried to ride it out.

Remy had suggested they share the sample platter, and Ash had avoided the spiciest, knowing his pale-Scot taste buds might not be up to scratch.

He grabbed a fry and shoved it into his mouth. It helped some… barely.

"You okay?" Remy stared at him wide-eyed and bit his lip.

"Aye," Ash wheezed and nodded. "I, uh, didnae mean to brave one of those." He coughed.

For a second, Remy's shoulders trembled and his lips pressed together. Then he gave up and burst into laughter. "Your face."

Ash scowled. "I'd like to see you do better." A fool's bet, of course.

Remy selected one of the fiery wings, then ate it all in one go. His eyes watered a bit, but he kept on.

Ash pouted. "No fair. We don't do hot in Scotland." At least not in the native fare.

Remy arched a brow. "Canadians aren't much better."

Ash studied him. He was willing to bet Toronto had as many options as Vancouver for takeout and groceries.

"But I didn't grow up in Toronto," Remy countered with delight. "Born in Quebec, and let me tell you, French Canadians don't do spice."

"Well, you learned to eat it somewhere."

Remy wrinkled his nose. "Mom is an excellent cook…."

Ash snorted and regarded Remy for a moment. "If you were raised in Quebec—"

"Oh. I wasn't. Mom moved us to Ontario when I was a baby."

"Oh. Here?" Ash tilted his head, curious.

"Nah, further east. I came here to do my master's." He shrugged. "Never lived in the GTA before—Greater Toronto Area."

"I know what it is."

"You really have gone native."

Ash snorted and didn't respond to that. "Do you like living here?"

"Hmm." Remy licked his thumb clean and shrugged. "It's all right. I like that it's big, that no matter what you're into, you can find something to do any given week. But, I don't know, I'm not connected to the city. Maybe too much non-Torontonian Ontarian bias," he laughed. "You may have noticed Ontario is divided: people who like Toronto and everyone else." He winked.

Ash snorted. He'd learned that within his first year living this side of the pond, even all the way out on the west coast. "You think you'll stay here after you finish uni, then?"

"Maybe. To be honest, it's about getting work. Basically I plan to go to whoever is willing to pay me." He wrinkled his nose. "That's still months away, though. Right now I have to worry about my thesis. Word of advice, if someone tells you it's a great idea to write a paper comparing different cultural treatments of werewolf mythology, they're wrong."

Ash snorted. "Are you not enjoying it?"

Remy shook his head ruefully even before Ash finished speaking. "I liked the topic—that's why I picked it—but everyone gets tired of their thesis. And mine might have been a bit overambitious, even after I decided to focus on film and TV. I've been consuming basically all I can in the last year, and trying to chart out the various depictions and attitudes." He shook his head. "Did you know Mexico had a fondness for werewolf films?"

"No."

"Well, they do, and I've watched many an hour of subtitled and badly dubbed movies to see what they have to say on the topic."

"And?"

Remy grinned. "You gotta read the thesis for that."

Ash snorted. Silence stretched between them. He ate another fry to occupy his tongue, but it still blurted out, "Was *Restraint* part of your research?"

"Dude, of course! No way I could talk about recent trends in North American media without including Zvi. Especially since *Restraint* went more shifter with their mythos, tossing out the moon stuff and focusing on the full shift and blending the human and wolf instincts."

That had always been one of Ash's favorite things about the character. Even in the later series, when Zvi had mostly been rehabilitated, he'd still put heavy emphasis on scent when interacting with others and tended to be more at ease when social hierarchies were clear. Half-man, half-wolf, Zvi was never at the mercy of it, never afraid of it. Ash wouldn't have loved Zvi the same if he'd been a monster.

"He's a big part of the whole section about using mythical monsters to expose humans as the true monsters. Not sure it'll make the final cut, but that's basically what Zvi is about, right?"

Ash inclined his head, his cheeks warming. He said the first thing that came to mind. "Who... what else you got in there?"

Remy munched a fry and considered. "Lately I've been focusing on comparatively recent stuff. Rewatched the Oz episodes of *Buffy*, did a marathon of the '80s films—*Teen Wolf, American Werewolf in London, The Howling*—oh, film three of Potter, new *Teen Wolf*." He wrinkled his nose. "Some of it's been fun. Some of it's terrible."

Ash laughed. He couldn't imagine consuming so much TV for research. "Why werewolves?"

Remy took a long drink of his iced tea, apparently considering the question. But surely others had asked him?

"I like werewolves? I mean, there are some pretty great stories out there." He shrugged. "I guess I liked how in a lot of those tales, they're born or made different. They can't help it. And not everyone can see how different they are at first, but no matter how hard they try to blend in, they always know they're not like everyone else." He shook his head. "Anyway, there's a lot of queer comparisons, and when you get a really good story, like Zvi, where his true 'otherness' comes from what other people have imposed on him? Well. I could really transfer all my gay angst onto that."

And there it was again. Remy simply dropping his sexuality into casual conversation, as though he had nothing to lose and no worries about how Ash would react to it.

"Oh." At a loss, Ash poked at his unused knife.

"Such as it was." Remy waved a hand in the air. "I mean, not that it didn't feel big and important, but looking back... I had it pretty good. Whiteish guy in Canada with a loving mom who honestly doesn't care? I didn't have too much to worry about when coming out, not compared to others. Still. I had my share of dramatic-sixteen-year-old moments." He smiled. "Anyway, Nisha and I were big into sci-fi when we were kids, and we were always drawn to the misfit characters."

Ash stared at him. He couldn't imagine being so… open. "How can you—? Aren't you worried about someone reacting poorly when you tell them?"

Remy stared at Ash for a long beat, his expression somber. Then he nodded once, decisive. "Sometimes I definitely hold back. But sometimes you get a feel for people." He shrugged. "I refuse to be afraid all the time. Besides, I've never met you before, but it's not like I haven't heard you say some queer-friendly things. Which I guess could have been PR, but I didn't think so."

He'd said queer-friendly things? Ash had the urge to cock his head like a bewildered puppy. Sure, he was careful not to sound homophobic, but he stayed away from the topic as best he could. He'd never been very publicly opinionated about anything, really. People didn't want him to be.

"Still." He looked away. "What if I wasn't alright? Aren't you afraid of being hurt?"

"Sure. Which is why I tend not to announce it on quiet street corners in the middle of the night." Remy smiled, but then after a beat, he dropped it. "Look. Not all the world is kind, so I'm careful, trust me. But generally speaking, there isn't much danger—given my situation— for me to tell someone in public in the middle of the day. If you'd reacted badly, I could have walked away, and we'd never see each other again. That would have been it."

Ash chewed his lip and considered Remy's open expression. It still sounded so… risky.

Remy stared back, his gaze searching. Wordlessly, Ash shifted his hips and scrunched a napkin.

Finally Remy spoke. "Everyone is different, but…. For me, I know I can probably make things a little easier on others who are less secure than I am. If my saying 'I'm gay' means someone else feels comfortable enough to say it back, or if it helps to make it more normal to hear? Well, I'm going to do it." He shrugged again but didn't quite achieve nonchalance. "I wish everyone felt comfortable enough to admit it, if it's true, but until then… I'll do my best. You know?"

Ash tore a few pieces off his napkin.

Across the table, Remy picked up and gnawed another wing, apparently content to sit in silence. Ash pushed a fry around his plate and wondered what Remy would say if he knew about him.

The Eurhythmics' "Who's that Girl?" started playing. Ash jerked, as did Remy. His eyes went wide, and he scrambled to get his hand into his pocket and yank out his phone. He swiped it clumsily and brought it to his ear.

"Nisha," he said too cheerily. "Hi. How are you?" His tone shifted to tentative. "Oh? Twenty…. That late, huh? … Um, so the thing is, uh, remember how I went to the ROM this afternoon? Well, I kinda—" Whatever her interjection, it made him blush. "What? No! Of course not. I met someone from out of town, and they were kinda… lost. So I gave them a hand, and then I guess I lost track of time."

He licked his lips, leaving them shiny, and then answered more slowly. "Yes. But that's not why—" He harrumphed. "It isn't."

His cheeks turned pink. "Yes." He was silent for a long moment. "Yes, tomorrow, I promise. I'll make it up to you." He hung up and slid his phone back into his pocket. Then he hunched his shoulders and avoided eye contact.

"All's well?" Ash asked.

"Yeah." Remy took a gulp of his Coke. "I totally forgot Nisha and I made plans to meet up for drinks tonight." He gave an *oops* face. "It's a good thing she'll forgive me after a couple of beers. Also listening to her bitch me out."

"She owns the Donna wig, aye?"

Remy's eyes widened a wee bit, and he nodded hard. "Yeah. She's my con buddy. Well, actually my everything buddy. I've known her since we were babies, complete with embarrassing photos of us bathing together."

Ash bit back a smile. Remy must have been an adorable child, all big eyes and wild hair. "So you're close, then."

"Oh yeah. She's the greatest. We're actually living together—well, for now. She and her true love are talking cohabitation." His shoulders slumped a little, but his smile didn't dim. "She got degrees in something much more useful—computer design and marketing. So she's working in tech and making, you know, *money*. She's also stupid smart and kinda my hero."

Ash would have sat and listened to Remy talk about his best friend in glowing terms for as long as Remy wanted, but his phone buzzed in his pocket, buzzed again, and then a third time.

Damn. Only one person sent him texts in rapid succession like that. He glanced at his watch and winced. It was almost nine, and he'd told Etta he wouldn't be out late.

He pulled his phone from his pocket. "My turn." He thumbed at the screen.

*Where are you?*
*Have you been murdered?*
*... are you having sex?*
*Please tell me it's the last one.*

Ash scowled, tilted his phone so Remy definitely couldn't see, and tapped out hastily, *No and No. Got caught up. I'll be back in under an hour.*

"Sorry. Etta, reminding me we've got an early flight tomorrow."

"Ah." Remy nodded. Then, "Do you mind if I ask something personal? I won't share it, I'm just curious."

Ash considered him. "I may not answer."

"Fair. Some of the fans think she's your girlfriend. But you two aren't dating, are you." It wasn't really a question.

Ash had heard the rumors and knew he benefited from them. So long as he had a plausible excuse for his not dating anyone else, his secrets were safer. And since Etta didn't care what his fans thought of her, he'd never done anything to address the speculation. But….

He didn't want to deceive Remy.

Ash shook his head. "No." He'd never dated anyone and certainly not Etta. "She's a good friend and a great bodyguard slash companion"—Remy's lips quirked—"but that's all."

Remy nodded, then smiled. "Well, I guess we better get the check, because I'm pretty sure I don't want on her bad side."

Ash nodded. "Yeah, she knows aikido and tae kwon do, and her current obsession is kickboxing." There was a reason, as a man over six feet, he'd been confident writing *bodyguard* on her employment contract.

Remy whistled. "Damn. Now I really want to get you home on time. I'm starting to worry for my own safety."

"As you should. She protects me from creepy fans," Ash said, straight-faced.

Remy chuckled and waved down their server.

"One bill," Ash said to Kayla, their waitress, and pulled out his credit card.

"No way—"

"Let me? I'm not in uni." He smiled, then added to soften the blow, "And I can write this off. This is a business trip."

Remy arched a brow. "This isn't exactly a business dinner."

"No. But my accountant adds up all the money I spend on these trips and does magic with the numbers. No reason to deny her extra fun."

After the bill was paid and they stood on the pavement once again, they stared at each other in awkward silence.

"So…," Remy said.

"Can I give you a ride?" Remy cocked his head, and Ash blushed once again. "A driver will be here soon to take me back to the hotel. I could give you a lift home."

Remy shook his head. "I'm like thirty minutes away from here."

Ash shrugged.

"I couldn't ask you to pay for that. *And* you're like ten minutes from whatever hotel you're staying at if it's near the convention center."

Ash shrugged again. "It's a car service. I'll be charged for an hour even if I don't take the full thing. Might as well use it."

After a beat, Remy finally nodded slowly in agreement.

When they got into the town car, the driver, Ray, asked where to, Remy gave an address, and Ray nodded, clearly familiar with it.

"You know," Remy said, casual, "I've never been in a service car like this before." He ran his hand over the plush leather seats. "Fancy," he whispered and winked.

Ash's lips trembled. He wasn't sure why such a silly moment made him want to laugh so much. "I guess so."

Remy smiled, leaned back, and then folded his hands over his belly. "I could get used to this."

"Well, once you've made it big on the *Times* best-seller list, you can afford a driver whenever you want."

"Oooh, good point," Remy said happily. "Hmm. Just gotta figure out what I'm going to write about. Vampires are passé, so best to avoid them, I think."

"Well, after all that research, wouldn't it be logical to write about werewolves?"

Remy hummed and turned to look at him, his head lolling on the headrest. "You think I should write about them, Mr. Werewolf?"

Ash smiled. "I only played one on TV...."

"Yuk, yuk," Remy said but not unkindly. He looked pleased. "So I shall write about werewolves.... Oh! I should write a book for kids—or preteens. The Harry Potter of werewolves. Maybe she goes to werewolf school."

"Werewolf school? What does one learn at werewolf school?"

"Hmm. Good question. How to Control the Shift? Lunar Cycles 101? How to Cook Rabbit? Fleas: How to Avoid Them and How to Remove Them?"

Ash's shoulders shook. "How to Howl?"

"Oh yes, definitely. Must-have for any young werewolf." Remy nodded seriously—if lazily—and tapped a finger to his chin. "Scent Marking: How to Pee a Little Bit?"

"Cats: Friend or Foe?"

"When Not to Lick Your Privates in Public?"

Ash let out a bark of laughter. "You definitely win."

"Oh good. I was worried about matching wits after I lost the dad-joke contest."

"I'm sure you were."

"Oh, I was. I'm known for my fantastic wit."

"Uh-huh." Despite his skeptical tone, Ash didn't doubt it.

"Yup," Remy said softly. He closed his eyes for a moment and hummed happily.

His eyelashes formed dark uneven crescents fluttering against his cheek. As they passed by storefronts, the changing lamps altered the shape of the shadows, and Ash contemplated the way the neons made Remy's tan skin more golden. It struck Ash of a sudden that he would never see him again.

Once Remy left the car, that would be it. Ash didn't have his number or email. There would be no more trips to charity shops or bakeries, and he would never get the opportunity to say hello or to send him a holiday or birthday card. This was it. The full extent of their acquaintance would span a weekend—or just over twelve hours, really. Ash's gut said it would stay with him. He wouldn't forget Remy, but he wouldn't ever see him again.

Remy still hummed softly. A couple of the bars sounded familiar, but Ash couldn't name the tune. Maybe he should ask what it was.

Or maybe he should ask for his number. Or an email. They could stay in touch. Ash was an adult. No reason he couldn't simply ask, couldn't say, "Remy, I like you. Why don't we keep in touch?"

But… there was one glaringly obvious reason. Fame, at any level, changed the rules when it came to meeting people and making friends. Ash was not mobbed every time he went out in public, but Remy was a fan. And though Ash stayed positive that Remy would never share today with the internet, he really had no way of knowing. Maybe Remy was a lie and he'd been saving up the details to tweet later.

Ash shouldn't ask him, shouldn't say anything.

But the thought of never talking to Remy again, not even once....

"We're here," the driver said and pulled the car to a stop.

Ash looked out the window and noticed they were at the entrance to a community of neat wee row houses. He blinked, then shook his head. Had he really wasted their last twenty minutes—

"Well, this is me." Remy was turned in his seat, facing Ash, and smiling. "Today was fantastic. Thank you. I had a great time. Total dream come true. Thank you." He unbuckled, opened his door, and gave a wee wave. "Toodles. Oh, and safe flight tomorrow." Then he stood and stepped out of the car.

Ash's tongue stuck to the roof of his mouth, his lips sealed shut. He swallowed and tried to think of something, anything, to say. *Thank you too? Goodbye? Don't go? Tell me your number before you leave me forever?*

Remy leaned down and peered through the open doorway. "Thanks for the lift. Both of you," he said more loudly for Ray. "Have a good one. Bye." Then he smiled one last time and closed the door.

Ash watched, mute, his lips forming the word *goodbye* several seconds too late, as Remy walked away from the car, his movements fluid and upbeat.

"Back to your hotel, sir?" asked Ray.

Ash nodded, not sure his voice would work. His hand fell from his chest—useless to touch the coin now. He craned his neck to watch Remy for as long as possible, until he disappeared behind a house and the car pulled Ash out of range.

And he was gone. For good. Out of Ash's life. And Ash had nothing, not even an address, since Remy had only given them a community, and Ash didn't hold out any hope for finding a listing for a student.

So. That was it. The end.

Ash sat back in his seat, closed his eyes, and tried to will away the stone pit lodging itself into his stomach. There was no use dwelling on what-ifs.

If only he knew how to stop.

*Part II*
*Vancouver*

## *Chapter One*

**"ASHLAAAND,"** Jasmine shouted and, when Ash reached striking distance, launched herself into his arms, her black ponytail streaking out behind her. He caught her easily, despite her height, and she wrapped her limbs round him in a full-body hug.

He took in a deep breath. She still smelled of honey and freshly baked goodies.

"It's so good to see you," she said with exuberance. "We got picked up. Can you believe it?"

"No," Ash said with a self-deprecating laugh. He really couldn't. He knew their pilot was gold, well-put-together on all fronts, and their showrunner had a résumé of success, but all that meant naught when it came to the television gods.

He might have been doing his best not to hope.

"But we did, and we're here." Jasmine pulled back and slipped gracefully from his arms. She brought grace to everything she did, though you wouldn't think it seeing her joggers and ball cap.

"Come on, Highlander—"

Ash rolled his eyes. "I'm from *Glasgow*." *Or close enough, to Americans.*

"—come say hello again to everyone."

She grasped his hand and pulled him to the table. Ash might have a natural un-Scottish bent toward shyness, but he wasn't wary of this group. He and his castmates had got on like a burning house during the week they filmed the pilot, and he was relieved to see them all again.

"Hey." Miya gave him an awkward finger wave. Her hair was pulled back in a messy bun, several locks falling into her face and sweeping in front of her large chunky black frames. She'd curled her petite form into her chair, a feat no one else there was likely to manage, and one knee poked out over the top of the table.

"Hallo," Ash said. "S'good to see you." He smiled for her, then turned to the other two members of their cast, Kim and Michael.

Michael, tall, dark-skinned, and beautiful, nodded and smiled in greeting. He lounged in his chair, looking very cool, a contrast to the boisterous energy Ash had often seen that first week. "So glad to see you again, *darling*."

Ash rolled his eyes. The Irish accent might charm the North Americans, but it didnae work on him.

"Guid tae see you too, cupcake." Two could play that game.

Kim snorted, one sardonic eyebrow raised. She hadn't put product in her short hair today, and her tawny brown fringe swept across her forehead. She was dressed down in flannel plaid and jeans, and pulling the look off well. "You two trying to practice the sexual tension?" she asked drily.

Despite himself, Ash's cheeks warmed. *That* was the number one reason he'd wanted this job: Hamish Dunbar was gay.

Michael grinned. "Of course. Nothing comes easy without practice."

Jasmine snorted. "As if your oh-so-obvious on-screen pining wasn't one of the number one likes of the pilot."

Miya nodded enthusiastically. "Yes. Janet told me it was very popular with the female viewers." Even when excited, her voice remained quiet.

Though he'd heard similarly from their showrunner, Ash scratched his new beard, self-conscious.

"Oh!" Jasmine clasped her hands in front of her chest. "They're going to make so many fan works about you two."

Having been half of a show's most popular 'ship before, Ash had seen some of the stuff fans could produce. People had gifted some pretty fantastic art to him and Adele. He even had one of Zvi and Moira framed on his wall.

He was proud to be part of something that meant so much to people, but the thought of being the center of that enthusiastic attention once again made him blush.

Michael didn't seem fazed, possibly because his résumé so far only consisted of guest roles. He smirked and said, "Well, I *am* very handsome and charming."

Kim rolled her eyes. "And it's all about you, of course."

"All right, children," Janet called. She stood in front of her chair and gestured about with her water bottle. "As much as it pleases me to see you all getting along so well, how about we get this table read started?"

"Hell yes," Jasmine crowed.

Janet smiled. "Thank you, Jasmine. First I want to welcome everyone, new and returning, to the table read for episode two of *Mythfits*."

Everyone cheered and applauded.

"Now, as we have a couple of new faces in the room, let's do quick introductions before we get underway."

They went around the table, and cast and crew alike gave their names and roles.

"I'm Miya, and I play the yokai weather spirit, Nariko." She gave a sweet smile and waved to everyone.

"I'm Michael, and I play the Irish fairy, obviously." Miya poked him. "Oh, Niall." He rolled his eyes at the name, but his lips quirked.

Kim went next. "I'm the otter shifter, Hana'a." She brushed her bangs out of her face.

Jasmine grinned and introduced herself as the "kickass vampire-lady, Roxanna."

Which left Ash, or "Hamish, the brownie."

"And love of my feckin' life, sugarplum," Michael interjected.

Laughter rose around the room, and Ash relaxed into his seat, smiling.

And so it began.

**"IT'S** everything I ever wanted," Ash told Langston later that night over the phone.

He hummed softly. "Yeah?"

"Ay. The script is *good*, it's funny and real, and my costars are amazing and talented." Ash fiddled with his coin, twisting it round the chain. "And—" He cleared his throat. "—my character is gay." He'd been reluctant to mention it before, but now that filming for the full series had started, it was time to tell.

After the longest few seconds of Ash's life, Langston said, "Really?"

"It's, uh, why I pushed for the audition." He'd ranted to Langston months ago about his agent calling it a waste of his time. Even if he could manage the comedy, no one would hire the brooding Zvi to star in a dramedy, fantasy-based or no. But not once had he mentioned that Hamish was openly gay from the first episode or that Niall the faerie and Roxanna the vampire had extremely fluid and flexible sexualities— not to mention the tentative noises the writers made about Miya's character being asexual.

"Really?"

"Aye."

"Oh. Are you planning on, er, 'coming out,' then? If you're playing this queer bloke on TV?"

"No," Ash said quickly, memories of too-trusting Sam intruding. "Definitely no'. No' ready for that. But Ah'm ready for this."

"Good." Langston huffed. "You know we'd support you, if you wanted—"

"Aye," Ash blurted, cheeks burning. He'd never doubted it, but better not let Langston finish that thought.

"Good. Ye numpty."

Ash snorted a laugh and said round the lump in his throat, "Thanks, roaster." After living in Canada for seven years and London for three before that, Ash had mostly trained the Scottish out of his everyday, but it always came back full-force with Langston.

"So. How are Fi and the girls?" Ash asked, desperate for the conversation change.

"Fit and fine as ever. Linsey says she's gonna be a ballet dancer, and wee Shona discovered paints. Her art is hanging everywhere. Fi says we'll have to start binning it soon to make room for more."

A soft noise escaped Ash. "Fi sent me a photo yesterday." He was so grateful for mobiles and Insta; without them he'd never see his nieces. "They're getting so big."

"Aye. That's what weans do."

"Shut yer gob," Ash said without heat. He and Langston were close as children, but when Ash moved away to acting school and then to Canada to follow a job—and maybe even to escape... something—the distance had done its inevitable damage.

A key turned in the front lock, and Etta walked in carrying a paper bag. Dinner had arrived.

"Etta brought me tea. Best say g'night," he said, watching her kick off her boots and lock the door.

"Alright. I'll tell Fi and the girls you say hello. Cheers."

"Cheers."

"How's the brother?" Etta asked as she transitioned into the kitchen. She settled on the other side of the counter and began pulling Indian out of the bag.

"Alright," he answered. "Smells well tidy."

Etta smiled at him, then turned to get plates. "You're always difficult to understand after you talk to him."

Ash rolled his eyes and made for the fridge. "Want a bevvy?" He poured a water for himself and grabbed a beer when she asked.

They settled at the breakfast bar and dished out food.

"How was the first day as a fairy?"

Ash paused, his fork halfway to the paneer dish, and gave her a look.

She shrugged. "Nope, it's never going to get old. I'll make that pun until I die."

Ash took a bite of paneer. "Numpty."

Etta narrowed her eyes. "If you think I don't know what that means after four years, then the only numpty here is you." She pointed a judgmental finger at him.

Ash grinned. "So, how was your day, dear?"

She rolled her eyes at the tired joke and reminded him that she'd spent much of her day watching his sorry ass—ouch—but then, as always, she shared some conversation, news from home, her trip to the gym.

The very best of traditions.

After they finished eating, he tidied up while Etta watched him, smirking. Then, because of their early start in the morning, they said good night and retreated to their bedrooms.

Ash curled up round his pillow and closed his eyes. With his heart made light by a new job and love from his brother, he fell into an easy sleep.

## *Chapter Two*

**"I WILNAE** make ye brownies," Hamish said in the firmest tone he could, which wisnae very.

"Not even for me, love?" Niall batted his eyelashes as he leaned across the counter.

"I dinnae make brownies for aught."

"Please?" Roxanne leaned in too, doing her best to look sweet and innocent. A remarkable feat for a 600-year-old vampire, but it was much less of one for Jasmine behind the mask.

"No. I'll no' be a cliché." Hamish sniffed and turned away—and Ash caught sight of a familiar face standing behind the camera. *Remy?* Ash froze, his heart hurried up, and his mind went blank. He hadn't thought—but here Remy was *on the set* of Ash's new job.

"Hamish? Darlin'?" Niall's voice cut through the fog of Ash's surprise, and he turned back to his costars, trying to remember what he was meant to be doing.

He licked his lips, then shook his head. He couldn't fake his way through this one. He was too rattled. Even though the lines came back to him, he'd too thoroughly blown the pace of the scene.

"Sorray," he said. "I, uh, dinnae ken what happened." He colored, suddenly embarrassed that he struggled to go in and out of Hamish's stronger brogue—even if he had to keep the accent lightish for American viewers—and that Remy was hearing him speak like this, as though he'd grown up in the Highlands a few hundred years ago and not outside Glasgow in the '90s.

"No problem," said Sophia, the director, a local Ash knew well from his days on *Restraint*. "Happens to the best of us. Let's take it from 'I won't make you brownies,' please."

Ash resettled in front of the counter, touched his pendant hidden beneath his costume, took a deep breath, and closed his eyes. When he opened them, Michael and Jasmine eyed him curiously, but he shook his head minutely, and neither of them asked. Then the director called action, and they started again.

This time Ash firmly ignored everyone behind the camera and made it through the scene... barely.

Once they'd finished the run-through, Sophia called it a wrap for the morning and sent them on their lunch break. Ash bit his lip and avoided eye contact, embarrassed to have scuppered a scene so completely.

Michael clapped a hand on his shoulder and tilted his head to the side. "Join us?"

Ash glanced about, but Remy no longer stood behind the camera.

He nodded. "Aye." Time alone wouldn't do him any good.

They gathered food from craft services and settled together to eat. Because Michael and Jasmine were fantastic people—and also fellow actors who understood—neither of them mentioned Ash's somewhat pathetic prelunch performance, and instead Jasmine launched into a story about her weekend trip to Banff with her boyfriend and dog, which soon had the others chuckling.

Before getting this job, Jasmine hadn't much television experience. She'd mostly worked in sketch and stand-up comedy and much of it for YouTube. At times she made her last gig obvious when she told one of her "you won't believe what happened to me last Saturday" stories.

He and Michael were still wiping away tears when Janet said, "Looks like I'd better hear this one."

Ash turned to her and his breath hitched. Remy stood with her, dimpling shyly at their trio.

Forewarning did nothing to dull the effect of seeing him. Ash looked down at his plate and took calming breaths.

"Definitely," Michael said with a chuckle. "Now, introduce us to your adorable shadow." Michael shot Remy a very flirty smile, and hot jealousy flared in Ash's gut.

"I'd love to." Janet beamed and waved a hand. "This is Remy Beaumont, newest addition to our writing team—part intern, part advisor. He's got a degree in magical monsters, so he's gonna help keep your backstories straight, as well as bring in different species of guest stars."

Ash managed enough courage to raise his gaze to Remy once again. He looked... God, better than he had months ago, which was terribly unfair. He had a longer hairstyle, which better suited his face, and new glasses with large frames that made his eyes pop.

Remy waved and smiled at them. "Hello."

Ash wanted to lunge across the table and kiss him. He looked away, surprised by the fierceness of the desire. His heart pounded.

"Remy, meet the lovely and hilarious Jasmine, the charming and beautiful Michael, and our shy and sweet Ash."

"Nice to meet you," Remy said to Jasmine and Michael, then turned to Ash and tilted his head, asking permission.

"We've already met," Ash's mouth said, surprising him almost as much as the others.

"You have?" Janet looked back and forth between them. "You never said anything," she accused.

Remy shrugged. "It wasn't a long acquaintance. I wasn't sure he'd remember, and I didn't want to sound like I was name-dropping for a job."

Janet chuckled. "As if you'd need to. You came highly recommended, and you're overqualified for the intern position as it is."

Remy grinned at the praise.

"So, will we see you around set much?" Michael asked, thankfully not fluttering his lashes or some such nonsense.

Janet nodded. "I want him here as much as possible at first, to get used to things, and then we'll see. Maybe on days with new creatures, so he's on hand to troubleshoot. No point in hiring that big brain if we're not going to use it," she added cheerfully.

"It's fun being on set," Remy said earnestly, with a little bounce. "I've never seen anything being filmed before."

Michael chuckled. "Hopefully you'll still feel that way after you watch us act out a scene twenty times in a row."

"Well, if each take gets the same care and variation as I saw earlier today, I don't see why not."

Had Remy always been so optimistic?

Janet laughed and slung an arm around his shoulder. "Come on, kid, you got more people to meet. Might as well quit this group while you've got them all charmed with your naïveté."

"It was nice to meet you." He smiled at Jasmine and Michael. "And to see you again, Ash. I like the new look," he called over his shoulder as he was dragged away.

Scruffing his beard, Ash watched him go, then turned back to his friends, who were watching him. Ash blushed furiously.

"Well," Michael said, "I want to know everything."

Judging from Jasmine's jerk and Michael's jump, she'd kicked him under the table—hard. "You don't have to tell us anything." She smiled kindly at him. "Of course, if you want to…."

Ash sighed. "There isn't anything to tell, really. I ran into him when I was playing tourist in Toronto last year. He was doing the same, and we tagged along with each other."

Michael hummed disbelievingly, but Jasmine nodded. "Good day, then?"

"Yeah," he said simply.

"What did you think of my hometown?" she asked.

"You're from Toronto?"

She shrugged. "Sorta. Came here when I was a kid. Grew up in the 'Greater Toronto Area.' Which means my parents couldn't afford to live in Toronto itself."

Ash snorted. "Well, I've been a couple of times because of the big convention. I didn't really get to see much of the city, though. What I did see was good." He tried not to think about being pulled into a supply closet with Remy or goofing around in the vintage shop or watching him eat wings.

"Ooh, do you think *we'll* do conventions together?" Jasmine asked, her eyes lighting up. "It would be so cool if we all went to the Toronto one, and then I could show you around my 'hood.'" She laughed.

Ash smiled. Jasmine and Michael would quickly become the benevolent rulers of any con, which suited Ash fine. He preferred the big cons, like San Diego or Seattle, because he never went alone. The *Restraint* cast went to either between series, and Ash hid behind Adele and Jonny every time.

Would it be too much to hope that their fantasy dramedy get the same promotion? That could be... good. Not only would Jasmine and Michael love it, but he suspected Miya would join him in geeky appreciation and Kim would lurk with him behind the extroverts.

Under the table, Ash crossed his fingers.

**ETTA** picked him up at the end of the day of filming, took one look at his face after he climbed in the car, and asked, "What happened?"

Ash swallowed. "Uh, so remember the time in Toronto when I went to play tourist by myself?"

Etta arched an eyebrow. "And you met an adorable out boy who you've been pining after ever since? I'm vaguely familiar."

Ash warmed. Sometimes he wished Etta didn't know him so well. "Well, he got hired as a myths-and-monsters specialist for the show. Janet wants him round set so he can learn and answer questions if needed."

"You're shitting me," Etta said. She hit the brakes a wee bit too hard at the traffic light and turned to him. Relaxing back into the seat and away from the seat belt, Ash nodded. "Jesus. Is geek boy stalking you? I know I said he was cute at the time and that you should bang him, but do I need to break him?" Her eyes narrowed menacingly. Behind them, someone honked their horn. "Yeah, yeah," Etta muttered, waving her middle finger over her shoulder and hitting the gas.

Ash cocked his head. "No. I don't think so. It's probably a coincidence. He'd mentioned wanting to use his master's to work on scripts."

"Hrm," Etta grunted and angrily flicked on her blinker. "Well, I'm following you into work tomorrow. I hope you know that."

"Etta...."

"No, I'm your bodyguard, which means I guard your body, which means I check up on cute boys who may be stalking you."

"You gonna do a background check too?"

"You know, that's not a bad—"

"I'm pretty sure studio security already took care of that," Ash hastily cut in. He hadn't meant to give her any ideas.

"Well, I'm still coming in tomorrow." She waved off his objections with a casual hand. "I'll bring my gym clothes, tell them I'm making use of their fancy actors' gym like they said I could."

"I appreciate your discretion," Ash said, monotone.

"No problem." She stopped at another intersection. "Now, am I turning left for sushi or going straight for pizza?"

"Straight," Ash said firmly. Today deserved pizza.

"Well, if we're breaking diet, I say we go all out. Phone in the order, and we'll stop at the IGA for some Häagen-Dazs." Ash didn't argue.

He stayed in the car while she dashed in for their ice cream—sometimes he wasn't in the mood to risk being spotted—and called for their favorite pizza.

Imogene laughed when he tried to give her their order. "The usual, right? Don't worry, we got it saved on file. It'll be ready in twenty minutes."

"Thank you." Ash made a mental note to add a wee bit extra to the tip.

After he hung up, he sat in the quiet, stared out the window, and watched the other grocery-store patrons hustle past the SUV. It was turning dark and had started to rain—unsurprisingly for April—so they were pulling hoods up and hurrying through the car park.

Ash hadn't thought he'd ever see Remy again. When he said goodbye to him last summer, he believed it for good. That knowledge, that he'd met a nice young man but had been too afraid to even ask for a number, caused Ash several nights' worth of deep introspection. He wasn't sure—naw, that wisnae right. He was *positive* he wouldn't be Hamish Dunbar right now if not for Remy.

Ash didn't know how to process that it wasn't over. He jiggled his leg.

How much time would he actually spend with Remy? Maybe they'd barely talk. Maybe Remy wouldn't actually be on set much; maybe Janet was wrong in her estimations.

He touched his coin.

Or maybe Remy would be there every day and Ash would get to talk to him during their breaks and—

Etta opened the door and hopped in. "Done. One Mint Chip and one White Russian procured. Tell me the pizza's waiting."

"The pizza is waiting," Ash said dutifully.

Two hours later they were camped on the couch, eating their ice cream and watching *Doctor Who*.

"So… are we gonna talk about it?" Etta asked.

Ash shoved a spoonful of mint chocolate into his mouth. He shrugged and swallowed. "Rather talk about how handsome Ten is."

"Hmm, yes, I know he's your favorite," Etta said. She waved a hand. She ate some vodka ice cream and contemplated the screen where David Tennant swanned about as the tenth Doctor. "He is pretty cute, though." She cast Ash a sideways look. "Cuter when he's still got the Scottish accent."

Ash wrinkled his nose. "Dinnae know about cuter, but he sounds like home." Ash had grown up only a few miles from Tennant.

"Huh. Does he make you homesick?"

Ash shrugged, mouth full of ice cream. "Wee bit."

"Oh."

They sat in silence for a while, and then Etta broke it. "Wasn't geek boy dressed up as Ten at that con?"

Ash froze. How did she remember? "How…?"

"Dude, he face-planted onto your dick. And you totally had a crush. Of course I remember."

Ash tried to hide his burning face in his ice cream.

Etta reached over and ruffled his hair. "You're so cute."

Ash narrowed his eyes and sullenly ate another spoonful. "Oh, shut yer gob and eat yer booze ice cream."

Etta laughed and did just that.

The next episode started, and Ash slumped further into his seat and tipped his head onto Etta's shoulder.

"He's really cute," Ash whispered, tired.

Etta grunted. "Your love for Ten has already been established this evening."

"Not Ten," Ash said. Then, after a pause, he managed, "Remy."

"Ooh, him. 'Cute,' eh?"

"Aye. Veray cute."

"You gonna be okay?"

Ash thought about that seriously. "Maybe," he mumbled.

Etta hummed softly and ran her fingers through his hair. "I think you will be. You're strong stuff."

Knackered, Ash hummed. "Thanks."

"No problem. Now shush. Tony Head's on the screen."

Ash snorted but did as he was bid.

## *Chapter Three*

**ASH** didn't see Remy for the next two days. Buzzing, he hung on tenterhooks at work, alternating between eagerness and dreading the idea of seeing him. When Ash wasn't focused on work and being Hamish, his mind feverishly ran through various scenarios. What would he say to Remy? What would Remy say in return?

By the end of the second day, on little sleep, Ash was shattered. On Friday morning he dozed in the car on the way to work and shuffled into makeup in a near-zombie state. As he noted the time, half eight, he was exceedingly grateful to no longer have regular 3:00 a.m. wake-up calls to be put into werewolf getup. Hamish took no prep. They even let Ash keep the new beard—something about all the ginger making him look more Scottish.

On the downside, the visit to makeup was so short he couldn't sleep in the chair.

As he made his way from costume to the set, he did his best to wake up. He was so focused on his shattered state, he failed to notice anyone else until he about stepped on them.

"Oh, sorry," Remy said in that cute, reflexive Canadian way.

Ash stared at him—the adorable nose, the new shaggy hair—and spoke a beat too late. "It's fine."

"Right. Still. Uh, so, hi." Remy awkwardly scratched the side of his nose. "Sorry."

Ash blinked. Surely if Remy had been *this* cute the last time, Ash would have remembered it. "It's, uh, good to see you," Ash said somewhat stiffly. "Again."

"Yeah. You too, man. I mean. Look, I hope you know that when I applied for this job, I had no idea you'd be here, and I wasn't trying to—"

"Aye, I know."

"—stalk you or anything—you do? Oh… good." Remy's shoulders dropped, and he shifted his weight side to side. "How have you been?"

"Good." Ash nodded several times. "Fine." After a long pause, he asked, "You?"

"Good. Great. I got my master's degree—obviously—and moved across country for an adventure and a job. Reliable income, yay." He smiled. "Feels good to no longer be a student."

Ash nodded. He remembered the elation of finally being free, of having a "real" job. "Yeah."

"Well… I guess I better let you go. You probably need to go to the set, and I should get back to the writers." He waved an explanatory hand toward the men's room.

"Right."

"Okay. Um, later." Remy gave a dafty wave and then left.

Ash stared blankly into space for several long seconds, then took a deep breath. That hadn't been... optimal. Not exactly a great reunion, but it was done with, the first meeting. No more mystery or wondering how Remy would behave with no one else around. Looked like Remy hadn't missed him. Of course he hadn't. Stupid to think—

After another deep breath, Ash composed himself and headed for the set. He and Miya were filming some "best friends" scenes today. He suspected the make-believe intimacy and care would do him good.

During the first break in filming, Ash sat in the director's chair labeled with his name and pulled out his phone. He clicked over to Etta's text chain and stared at it for a long moment before he typed. *Talked to him again.* He considered what else to say. *Not the worst thing ever.*

She answered a minute later. *What every boy wants to hear. "Not the worst."*

Ash sighed and tucked his phone back into the pocket hanging off the side of the chair.

"All right, Ash, Miya, if you could get back on scene." They'd redressed—apparently sitting on the couch without props looked weird, so now they were at the kitchen table, where two mugs and a plate of cookies were set out. Ash eyed the treats—and their many calories—suspiciously.

The director waved them into their seats and toward the cookies.

Ash chewed his lip. Should he mention…? "Um, Hamish never bakes for hi'self, ye ken?" In the old lore, brownies did housework for food, especially of the calorie-heavy variety, so Hamish disliked baking for himself. It should be compensation, or a gift. Besides, according to the pilot, he and chocolate didn't mix.

The director narrowed her eyes, like she thought Ash was Difficult.

"He's also allergic to chocolate." He looked again at the chocolate chip cookies.

The director rolled her eyes and muttered a "Why?" and Ash didn't say, "Because the writers couldn't resist a brownie who couldn't stomach brownies." Instead he shrugged and looked as innocent as possible.

Miya's lips twitched as she pinched them together, clearly wanting to laugh in his face. Ash loved filming with her.

She, like the rest of their costars, was stupidly talented. When the cameras were off, she was sweet and bubbly, but when the director called action, she turned into a fierce and intimidating weather demon. She had the ability to make your guts quiver with one look. And Ash wasn't immune, for all he was three times her size. Fortunately Hamish had nothing to fear from Nariko the elemental and adored her more than anyone on earth, even when her black moods brought the rain.

Right then Hamish's headspace had less doubt and more overwhelming contentment from taking care of his best friend.

At times like this, Ash loved his job.


**ASH** hated his job. He was outside in the middle of another dreich Vancouver night, with the added bonus of an April chill, and soaked to the bone, all the while having to pretend to be excited and happy about his circumstances. Stupid brownie lore about helpful nighttime workers who could be bribed with honey. Ash didn't even like honey.

Stupid light Vancouver rains—so like those of the Isles—that didn't show up on camera but left you cold and wet.

Ash shivered under his umbrella and glumly waited to be called into the scene. He'd find a smile when the cameras were rolling.

"You look miserable," said a familiar voice.

Ash turned to see Remy a few feet away, dressed in a raincoat and wellies and holding an umbrella and a travel mug. He looked dry. Ash probably looked like a drowned rat. Well-good.

"Am drookit"—he shifted unhappily in his wet clothes—"and it's a wee bit baltic," Ash grumbled. "It's like being in Scotland." *But without the perks.* The only drawback to Vancouver. If it was gonna rain for half the year, it should at least have the benefits of proper comfort food. He'd kill for some stovies or tablet.

Remy snorted. "You're like a grumpy Scottish cat, indignant about being wet."

Ash gave him a baleful look. He was in Chucks and jeans because Hamish wouldn't wear wellies, or so Ash had been told very passionately by the costume department. He wasn't sure why they fought to keep the Chucks, given the damage the damp must be doing.

"Oh geez. Put those eyes away, will you? I feel bad enough already…." Remy sighed. "Now I wanna wrap you in a blanket too." *Too?* "Here. I got you hot tea from craft services." He held out the travel mug Ash hadn't been eyeing jealously and waggled it.

Ash blinked at the offering. "Really?"

"Yes, really. Now hurry up and drink it before you're called back."

Not waiting to be told twice, Ash snagged the mug, popped the top open, and took a careful sip. Oh God, it was so guid. Normally Ash would snark at a body for bringing him a cup of bloody *Scottish breakfast*, but right now he didnae care. The familiar brew was so comforting. He wished he had both hands free to wrap around the warm cup.

"Thank you," he said sincerely once he finally managed to remember his manners. His maw would be ashamed of the delay. "Really, thanks. Am better already."

"Good," Remy said. He gripped his umbrella handle in both hands while he watched Ash drink. "So, uh, how goes the filming?"

Ash's shoulders slumped. "No' so good. Damn the writers for having a scene outside and at night."

Remy gave an awkwardly wee cough. Ash groaned internally. Hello, mouth, meet foot.

"The scene is guid," Ash hurried to say. "Well-guid. Lots of great character development for Hamish, and it's really... guid." He stumbled to a halt, then took a deep gulp of tea. Why was he such an awkward mess?

He shot a glance Remy's way and found himself on the end of an assessing look. Head tilted to the side with a speculative air, Remy seemed to be deciding something.

"You really hate the rain, don't you?"

"Naw," Ash said stubbornly, then relented. "I cannae stand being in wet clothes."

"Oh." A smile pulled at the corners of Remy's mouth and made his lips tremble.

"Say it." Ash sighed. Whatever was bursting to get out couldn't be worse than his speculation.

"I'm sorry," Remy said around a giggle. "It's only, I didn't know two hundred pounds of Scottish manly man could be so adorable."

That... was not anything like what Ash expected. *Adorable*? He eyed Remy's smiling face. Was he being mocked?

"Probably for the best. It is, after all, what makes Hamish work so well."

Ash frowned. "Whit do ye know about my Hamish?"

"Dude, I've seen you film some scenes."

"No' many like."

"No. But I've seen the pilot—right after I got the job—and it's possible they sent an early cut of episode two my way."

Wait, Remy had seen episode two? "How's it look?"

"So good," Remy gushed. "Like, it didn't have the musical cues, and some of the transitions were rough, but this show is so funny, and it's only gonna get better."

"Ye ken?"

Remy stared at him for a moment, then shook his head. "Sorry, I—Hamish's accent always throws me off. Especially when it's coming out of Ash."

Should Ash be insulted? "It's no' far off how I sounded as a wee lad." His voice was as dry as the rest of him was wet.

Remy nodded. "No, I'm sure it isn't. But you don't anymore. You also sound a little English, a little Canadian. No one else sounds like you." Remy looked away and cleared his throat.

That was.... Ash didn't know what to make of it. They stood in awkward silence for a moment. Ash wished he knew what to say. He had never been a natural conversationalist, and clearly, sometime during the intervening months, he'd lost his ability to speak to Remy. He'd lost the comfort he felt during their runaway day and the learned skills he frequently dusted off to talk with strangers. For the third time since Remy arrived in Vancouver, Ash stared dumbly at him and wondered how to form sentences.

Ash took a sip of his tea. If his mouth was full, he wouldn't have to talk. Also, comforting warmth.

"Ashland! Here you are." Bob, the director this week, strode toward them. "Hiding under your umbrella? We're ready for you."

"Okay, let me…." He waved his tea and then tilted it back so he could quickly drink the rest. He shifted awkwardly for a second, wondering where to put the empty mug.

"Here." Remy held out a hand. "I can take it, bring it back."

Ash handed it to him. "Ta for the tea."

Remy smiled.

"Keeping the talent happy, are you?" Bob said jovially. He clapped a hand on Remy's shoulder. "Good work, kid. You'll fit in fine in this business if you've already figured out how to manage the actors." He chuckled. "Let's go, Ashland."

Ash's stomach dropped. He glanced at Remy's face but couldnae read it. Was that what Remy had been doing? Ash hadn't thought Remy the manipulative type, but it struck him suddenly how little he actually knew him. They'd only spent one day together.

Ash said nothing and turned to follow his director.

## *Chapter Four*

**ASH** paused on the pavement corner, hands on his hips, and stared up at the street sign. Panting, he silently cursed himself. When he woke up on his day off to discover sunny April weather, he'd decided to go for a run. And somehow he got turned round. Apparently seven years living in a city counted for nothing when put up against Ash's sense of direction.

He was also seriously regretting his commitment to his iPod. It still worked and was less bulky than his phone, so he preferred it for running soundtracks, and it also had the added bonus of making him unreachable—but the definite disadvantage of leaving him without GPS.

Ash scrubbed a hand through his hair. He had no idea which way was home. He wondered if he could get out of this without asking a stranger for directions. Vancouver was a big city, so the odds for him picking someone who recognized him were probably low, but he didn't want to talk to strangers. Especially not with his recognizable and eye-catching ginger hair uncovered.

He tapped at his pendant, not that he expected the coin to bring him luck just then.

"I Need a Hero" was midchorus when Ash turned, looked south—or maybe east?—and spotted a familiar figure.

For a long moment, he weighed the pros and cons of admitting to Remy he'd got lost in the city that was his second home.

Then Remy looked over and saw him. A smile transformed his face, and he lifted a hand to wave.

Figuring he'd give in to the inevitable, Ash jogged over and pulled the buds from his ears, cutting Bonnie Tyler off.

"Hey," Remy said loudly. "How are you? What are you—oh, running, right." He waved to take in Ash's gear.

Ash nodded, unsure what to say. He'd barely seen Remy since the night shoot earlier that week.

Remy looked away, cleared his throat, and turned back. "Look, the other night, I think maybe…. The director said something kinda assholey, and I wanted to make sure you didn't think I brought you tea to, like, make you more biddable." He swallowed. "I was trying to be nice. Anyway you've probably forgotten about it, but…." He shrugged.

Ash stared. The tight knot in his chest eased, and he cleared his throat. "No, uh, thank you. People act odd," he blurted. "When they know you're even a wee bit famous, they start being weird."

"Oh." Remy's shoulders drooped. "Well, I hope I haven't—"

"No," Ash rushed to say.

"Because I would hate for you to think I cared about that. I mean, I know this probably sounds totally stupid because of how we met, but I don't. Care, that is."

"No. Yeah." Ash swallowed, throat dry, and once again wished he knew what to say.

The silence stretched between them. Remy scratched at his nose, and Ash admired his long fingers and the curve of his delicate wrist.

"So," Remy said. "You must live around here if you're running in the neighborhood."

Ash had completely forgotten his predicament. His exertion-flushed cheeks grew warmer. Desperately he wished for a way out of the conversation, but no pits opened below his feet or angels descended from the heavens to point the way home. Time to be a big boy.

"I'm, um, not actually sure." Ash wrinkled his nose. "To be honest I wasn't focusing on my route, and I don't have my phone."

Remy's lips twitched. "Are you saying you're lost?"

Ash sighed and wished his cheeks were not so pale. Stupid ginger skin. "Wee bit," he admitted.

"Oh," Remy said through stiff lips, clearly still trying to keep the laughter at bay.

Ash sighed.

Shoulders shaking, Remy pulled his phone from his pocket and opened up Maps. He turned the phone so Ash could read it more easily.

"You are here," Remy said with a flourish.

Ash stared at the map, glanced at Remy, then reached out to touch the screen and widen the view. Shit. He'd run much farther than expected.

"Bollocks." He considered the route he'd have to take home again and, for the first time in a while, lamented that he always went running without his wallet. A cab might have been nice.

"You going to be able to find your way home again?" Remy chuckled.

Ash hated to admit his lack of surety, but remembering directions was also not a strong suit.

"Well." Remy licked his lips. "If you don't mind playing tour guide"—his lips twitched—"I wouldn't mind lending you the use of my phone." He waggled it in the air.

Ash considered the offer. "Tour guide. Right now?"

Remy shrugged. "I can walk you home… or to a neighborhood you know, and then collect on the tour-guide favor later. You know, at a time when you're not in sweaty running gear." He slowly ran his gaze over Ash's outfit, and Ash felt… seen, exposed. A shiver ran up his spine. He was pretty sure he liked it.

"How about lunch?" Ash blurted. "Get me home, and I'll change and take you to lunch." The walk would be one of the longest cooldowns Ash had ever taken.

"You're on!" Then he held out the phone again so Ash could read it. "Which way first, o fearless leader?"

**FOR** a brief moment, Ash considered dropping Remy off at a coffee shop in the neighborhood of his condo and not showing him where he lived, but he quickly realized he was acting a right dunderheid.

He let Remy into the flat and waved him toward the sitting room.

"Have a seat. I'll only be a mo."

Remy settled onto the sofa, pulled out his phone, and dangled it in the air. "I'm good. You go shower." He leaned back with a wiggle, evidently getting comfy.

Ash left him. He grabbed some jeans, briefs, and a henley, and then ducked into his en suite for the fastest shower. He was dressed and walking into the living room in under ten minutes.

His back to Ash, Remy was bent over to get a look at the books arranged on one of the lower shelves of the built-ins. They were one of Ash's favorite features of the place—on either side of a bay window sat floor-to-ceiling bookcases. He was especially grateful for them right then, as they facilitated a spectacular view of Remy's round bum.

*You perv, stop ogling without permission.*

Nervously Ash stepped closer and ran his hand through his damp hair. "Hey."

Remy straightened and turned, his face already full of a wide grin. "Hey! You're all clean, I see. That was fast."

Ash shrugged. Twitchy, he pushed up the sleeves of his shirt. "Practice." He licked his lips and glanced at the clock. *Almost noon.* His stomach rumbled audibly.

"Sounds like you're ready to eat. Man, you must be famished after your run. Should we go find a place?"

Ash hesitated. He didn't hate the idea of going out with Remy, of sitting down with him in a restaurant— *like a date*—but he wanted to stay in his space at the moment.

"Or we could stay in and grab something to eat here?"

Remy considered him and then nodded. "Okay." He waved Ash toward the kitchen end of the open-concept space. "So you gonna wow me with your culinary skills?"

A small coal of shame burned in Ash's stomach. He wished he could. He and Etta had a long-standing obsession with the Food Network, and during his second year on *Restraint*, he'd decided to learn to cook. Over the years, he'd hung on to the notion, and "learning to cook, proper like" had become one of those "someday" life goals. As such, he had at his disposal a functional kitchen fully stocked with appliances and tools, cookbooks, and spices. He did not, however, have very many skills with which to use them.

Still, he could make a decent brekkie of eggs, toast, bacon, and fruit.

He pulled out ingredients.

Remy eyed up the appliances on his countertops and opened a couple of drawers. He whistled at the knives hanging on the back wall. "Damn. You're giving me kitchen envy. I moved in with someone advertising for a roommate, and she doesn't have anything like this in hers. It drives me a bit nuts trying to use the space, actually. There's no room, and it's missing nearly all the stuff I need."

He spun and watched Ash turn the heat on underneath a frying pan. He cocked his head as Ash pulled out the butter.

"Can I help with anything? I'm an excellent veggie slicer."

Ash shrugged. "Naw. Was going to scramble eggs."

Remy frowned, but there was a stubborn lilt to his mouth. "No veggies?"

Ash shook his head.

"Okay. I know I saw vegetables hiding in that fridge."

He honestly wasn't sure what Remy expected him to do *with* the veg in his fridge. Most of them were for making salads. Etta was big on salads.

"Sorry? I'm not that great in the kitchen—"

"But," Remy exclaimed and made wide sweeping motions to take in the room, "this kitchen is amazing."

Ash put the butter down on the counter, an excuse to avoid eye contact. "I, erm, never really learned how to use it."

"What?" He sounded appalled.

Ash peeked over. Remy's mouth hung open. "I want to, but I've never really had the opportunity...." He ended with another shrug.

"Right. Okay. Shift over, let me at your fridge. I'm not eating sad eggs when you have this setup. We are eating omelets."

Remy put his hands on Ash's hips and shifted him over. His touch burned and sent tingling shivers all through Ash's body. Ash heated and his brain stalled. He'd never been so close to another man outside of acting or family.

Meanwhile Remy was apparently oblivious to the turmoil he'd left in his wake. He opened the fridge and started inspecting vegetables and muttering to himself, completely uninterested in Ash, which, Ash berated himself, was a good thing.

Trying to regain composure, he turned away and flicked the dial to turn the hob off. Didn't look like they'd be needing it yet.

By the time Remy settled his armload of veg on the counter, Ash was ready to face him again.

"All right. I need a cutting board." He looked at Ash with raised eyebrows, and Ash pointed. "Okay, so, first we need to wash things." He passed Ash the pepper, a tomato, and some mushrooms. "Do I need to give you instructions on how to clean those?"

Ash narrowed his eyes. "That is my fridge, you know. I did buy these"—Etta bought them, but it was mostly with his money, so semantics—"and have made salads before."

Remy held up his hands as if in defensive apology, but he didn't sound contrite in the least when he said, "Okay, okay, just checking. Wash those. I'll get started on the garlic and onion." He turned to the knife rack and rubbed his hands together gleefully. "Come to Papa, my pretties."

It should have been creepy, but instead it filled Ash with overwhelming fondness.

He scrubbed the pepper and tomato, then diligently cleaned the mushrooms of any dirt remnants—he kinda wished he'd never learned where they grew—and listened to the tap-tap of Remy's knife. It started off slow but turned into a flurry of sound. Ash looked over and saw Remy expertly mincing a clove of garlic. His long-fingered hands manipulated the knife with a competency Ash had only ever seen on cooking shows.

Ash swallowed hard and wished suddenly and fervently that he didn't have an embarrassing crush on Jamie Oliver, or that Remy wasn't doing such a fine impression.

Ash turned back to the mushrooms. If the next one looked especially attacked and bedraggled after he was done with it… well, Remy needn't know why.

Task completed, Ash turned round in time to see Remy dice the last of the red onion. It was still stupidly hot.

Remy looked up. "All done? Perfect." He scraped the onion into a bowl—and when had he gone looking for that?—put the board back on the counter, and waved Ash over. "Your turn."

"What?"

"Show me your chopping skills, dude."

Ash wrinkled his nose. "Nowhere near good as yours."

"Hmm, I didn't think they would be. Not when you said you didn't know how to use this stuff. But show me what you got, I can give you some pointers."

He handed Ash the pepper. Nervous—he hated an audience when he didn't know what he was doing—he chopped roughly at the pepper.

"Dude," Remy exclaimed, affronted. "Don't tell me this is how you cut everything."

"Er. Maybe?"

"Okay, no. First of all, your grip is wrong. Can I have the knife for a second? Look. Like this." Remy curled three fingers around the handle and gripped the blade between thumb and forefinger. It looked hazardous. "You have better control if you hold the blade. You try." He handed it back, and Ash tried to mimic him. "Better. I'm going to fix your hold. So keep still so I don't run into the blade, please."

Remy placed his hand over Ash's, and only terror at the thought of dismembering him allowed Ash to curb the impulse to jump, to jerk away. His heart rabbited.

"Perfect," Remy announced after he'd shifted Ash's thumb. He released his grip, and Ash wanted to shiver when he brushed his wrist. "Okay, now on to How to Hold Your Vegetable—and that sounds way dirtier than I intended," he laughed. "Seriously, though, if you hold it like this—" He placed his fingertips on the pepper and then curled his hand overtop. "—you never have to worry about taking out a finger. It also means you can eventually pick up speed." He grinned. Ash's insides did somersaults.

Not wanting to look a gift cooking lesson in the mouth, he focused on the pepper and did his best to ignore the heat of Remy at his side. He tried to mimic Remy and started cutting.

"Nice," Remy said softly and encouragingly. Ash shivered.

"Thanks," he croaked and looked over—and was instantly caught in Remy's gaze. For a long, agonizing moment, they stared at each other. Remy licked his lips and they shone.

Desperate to break the spell, to force Remy out of his space, Ash cast about for a distraction. "How do you know all this?"

"Oh, uh, my mom's a chef." Remy stepped back, and Ash nearly sighed with relief. "She's got her own restaurant now. But when I was a little kid, she worked part-time, and so she was around more for dinner. She taught me everything she knows." He let out a wee sigh. "Damn, I miss her cooking."

"She live in Toronto?"

"Nah, she's east of there. I grew up about two hours down the 401. Mom and Stepdad are still there. When I was studying in Toronto, I used to drive home to the restaurant on weekends for Mom's food. But can't exactly do that now. I have a lot of her recipes, but it's not the same."

Ash pushed away old memories—he'd been fifteen the last time he had his maw's home cooking—and nodded.

"Anyway." Remy cleared his throat. "All chopped up? Perfect. Now, I need a whisk, an egg flipper, and some spices."

Ash crossed the kitchen and opened the cupboard with the spices, then reached to open the drawer with the whisk and flipper. When he turned to hand them to Remy, he found him openmouthed and staring avidly at the spice rack.

Remy reached out and began fondling the labeled containers. "Damn. Why do you have this collection if you don't cook?"

Ash narrowed his eyes, starting to feel judged. "I told you I want to… and anyway, Etta likes making salad dressing."

"Right. Okay. Well, how do you feel about a spicy omelet? Or maybe something with less heat?" His lips twitched. "What about some oregano? Hmm, or maybe basil…?" He grabbed a couple of spices and set them on the counter.

He turned on the hob and glugged oil into the frying pan, his thumb over the spout like Jamie Oliver did. Ash swallowed.

Next Remy pulled a bowl from the cupboard, cracked some eggs into it, and whisked them briskly. He checked the pan, then scraped the veg from the cutting board, and they sizzled on contact. He looked confident as he moved—comfortable and without hesitation. Ash second-guessed every action in the kitchen.

Before long Remy added the spices, then the eggs, and ordered Ash to make toast.

"Oh! We forgot about the bacon." Remy threw a guilty look in Ash's direction.

Ash shook his head. "As if we need more food when you're making that." He nodded at the extra-large omelet, which was almost done.

Remy scratched his nose. "Well, if you're sure. Only it wouldn't be done on time if we started it now."

Ash pointedly put the bacon back in the fridge. "Etta will be pleased to discover it's still there later."

Remy found plates and served them each half the omelet and added the toast. They settled at the breakfast bar with their meal and glasses of orange juice.

Ash took his first bite of egg and moaned. They were heavenly. He quickly cut another, forked it into his mouth, and let out more noises of delight. Delicious. "This is fantastic." He turned to see Remy had turned red under the compliment. "Truly, it's the best omelet I've ever had. Ever."

Remy smiled and shook his head. "Thanks. It's kind of a specialty of mine. Full of protein and vegetables. I make them an embarrassing amount, actually." He wrinkled his nose adorably and then finally took a bite. He gave a thoughtful-sounding noise of satisfaction.

"Feel free to make them for me anytime," Ash said earnestly, "because these are amazing."

Remy glowed. And then Ash's brain caught up with his mouth and he realized he'd invited Remy to cook for him more often, to be here again. Should he clarify he hadn't meant to insinuate anything? But doing that would make things awkward, surely. He shoved another bite of omelet into his mouth, the better to keep it silent.

They didn't talk while they cleaned their plates. Ash was always starving after a run, and with food this delicious, he saw no reason to slow down.

He was seriously considering licking his plate clean, when Remy let out a snort.

"If you're that hungry, I can make you another."

Ash looked up. Remy was smiling and apparently had been watching him eye up his crumb-filled plate. It was Ash's turn to blush.

"No, no, it's fine. I'm full. Only... it was really good."

"Yeah, I got that." Remy's smile turned soft and genuine. "Seriously, I could make another."

Ash shook his head. "You're my guest. I shouldn't be making you cook for me."

Remy waved him off. "I offered, remember. I was the one who basically told you I could do better than you. And now I think about it, how about you forget that happened and that I was such a shitty guest?"

Ash laughed. "Alright." He stood and gathered up his dishes. Remy moved to follow, but Ash waved him off and swiped his dirty plate. "No. You made me brunch. Forget about it, I'm not letting you wash up."

Remy held up his hands. "I won't argue. Always hated washing dishes."

Ash shrugged. He'd always enjoyed tidying up and wasn't bothered. While Remy watched, he scraped off the plates, loaded them into the dishwasher, and then tackled the frying pan. He was scrubbing it free of egg when Remy hopped off his stool. He wandered down the length of the counter and stopped in front of the shelf of cookbooks.

He hummed as he read the titles. "You a fan of Jamie Oliver?"

God, would Ash ever stop blushing today? "Etta and I watch a lot of Food Network." He scrubbed harder at the pan.

Remy stepped toward him. "Okay. But I think you got the full Oliver oeuvre."

Ash couldn't read his tone, and he wasn't sure he wanted to look.

"Oliver's your favorite, then?"

Ash shrugged a shoulder. "I guess."

Remy fell quiet, and Ash finally stole the courage to look. Remy was creeping closer, head cocked.

"You're blushing," he gasped with delight. "Ohh. Do you have a mancrush on Jamie Oliver?"

Ash's cheeks burned brighter. "I do not," he said indignantly, which was the truth. He didn't have a *man*crush.

"You do. That's adorable!" Remy smiled again. Ash was as helpless under that grin as all the others.

Ash huffed and scowled at the now-clean frying pan.

"Aw, I'm sorry. Is it like fight club? First rule of the Jamie mancrush is we don't talk about the Jamie mancrush?" Ash looked over at him to arch his eyebrows, and Remy raised his hands in surrender. He licked his lips. "You know, if you wanted to learn to cook, I could teach you some things?"

"Could you?" Ash had aimed for disaffected, so his earnest tone surprised him.

"Of course. I'd be happy to come over and help you work through some recipes. Though I do have a heavy cost." His expression turned somber. "I expect to help you eat everything we make."

Ash tilted his head and tapped a damp finger to his chin. "Hmm. I thought I'd boot you out once the food was made. I'm no' sure I want tae feed you."

Remy gasped and placed a hand on his chest. "Scandalous, sir. No food, no lessons."

Ash heaved a great sigh. "Fine. If you insist, I can let you get a few bites to your gob."

Remy snickered. "My *gob*?"

Ash rinsed the pan and grabbed a tea towel to dry it. "Are you mocking my use of Scottish?"

"Scottish is a language now?"

"Aye, 'tis. An' no' just 'noo,'" Ash said, accent getting thicker for this fight. "Scots dinnae spake English."

"Oh my God," Remy breathed, clearly delighted. "I've never heard you sound so Scottish before, not even as Hamish."

Ash wrinkled his nose. "By-product of being 'good' at accents." His language-and-diction coach at school had called him a "natural mimic." He'd played English on British TV and American on *Restraint*. "I didn't realize how Canadian I started to sound until I went back." He snorted at the memory. "By the time I got a cab from the airport, I'd forced myself to sound like a Scot again." Ash leaned back against the counter and contemplated Remy for a second before adding, "My brother loves to mock me for 'speaking Canadian.'"

Remy cocked his head. "You don't sound Canadian."

"Aye, but I don't sound full Scottish either, as you've already told me. Though when I talk to my brother, it comes back. But some words always come out 'Canadian.'"

"Like?"

"Hmm, place names. Words we don't use in Scotland." Ash shrugged. "He thinks it's funnier though when I use Canadian terms, like if I say *garbage* instead of *bin*."

Remy nibbled a lip. "I never noticed before that you do, say *garbage*, I mean."

"To be honest I got tired of the confused looks."

Remy laughed. "Poor you! Having to deal with unworldly Canadians." He stepped closer, smiling up at Ash—had his lashes always been that long?

Ash sighed dramatically and nodded. His life was indeed hard.

And it was about to get harder, because Etta called from the front door, "Honey, I'm home."

Ash froze. He'd forgotten Etta would be back after lunch. He glanced at the clock—almost one. He considered how close Remy was stood. Oh God. This wouldn't go smoothly.

"Hello," Etta purred. She stood on the other side of the breakfast bar, looking Remy up and down, a cat eyeing prey. "And who do we have here?" She lifted a brow at Ash.

"Hi." Remy's tone was warm, despite the trepidation around his eyes. "I'm Remy. I work on *Mythfits* with the writers."

"Ohh." She cocked her head and gave him a blatant once-over. Ash sweated, rooted to his spot near the sink. Unable to…. *Could* he stop this? "You look familiar. Have we met before?"

"No? Well, I mean, I met Ash at a con months ago, and you were there, but we didn't talk, and I wouldn't expect you to remember me."

Etta widened her eyes in faux realization. "Oh. You're not the one who put Ash in the wig, are you?"

"Yes?" Remy said warily.

"I have a picture." Etta smirked.

Remy's eyebrows flew to his hair. "You have a picture of me?"

"I have a picture," she said slowly, with narrowed eyes, "of Ash in a wig. You just happen to be in it."

Remy lifted his hands in surrender—wise man. "Fair enough."

"So," she said, leaning against the counter. "What have you boys been up to today?" She turned to Ash.

That question had so many layers. Primary were her concerns about Remy's interest. She had yet to be convinced he wasn't a stalker. Ash glared. He did *not* need protecting from Remy.

She pointedly ignored him and turned back to Remy, who shrugged.

"Haven't made up our minds yet. Just had some brunch. Maybe we could go for a walk around the neighborhood?" he directed at Ash, who quickly dropped his scowl.

He nodded. "Sure."

Remy smiled. "Perfect. Would you like to come too, Etta?" His tone was perfectly polite, nothing to suggest he wanted her to do anything but what she desired.

Ash's renewed glare was not so, and he did his best to ramp it up. Etta was no' invited to join them.

She cocked her head to the side and then smiled. "As much as I would love to join you, I spent the morning at kickboxing. I promised myself I'd start the afternoon in the bath. Have fun, boys. And you"—she pointed at Ash—"put those groceries away."

Ash rolled his eyes but dutifully fetched the bags she'd left by the door, like always. She said it built character for him to carry the bags through the flat, given she'd lugged them all the way home. It sounded a load of mince to him, but it was easier to do as told than argue about the difficulties of "lugging" groceries by car.

Remy shuffled over and peered inside a bag. "Want a hand?" He didn't wait for a reply but pulled items from it.

"Thanks." Then, feeling the need to explain away Etta's behavior, Ash said, "She does more of the grocery runs when I'm working."

Remy nodded. "Makes sense." He smiled and handed Ash a bag of apples to put away.

Ash smiled back. It was… nice, this quiet moment shared. Soon they would get ready and head out for a walk and there would be strangers about them. But for the moment, it was only them, and Ash could get used to it.

## Chapter Five

**"SOMEONE'S** happy today," Jasmine said cheerfully and threw her arm around Ash's shoulders and leaned into him. She wore Roxanna clothes—tight black jeans, an overlarge black jumper, thick smudged eyeliner, and her long hair down and straight, framing her face—a sharp contrast to her sunny smile.

Ash lifted his eyebrows.

"You've been smiling all morning. You wake up on the right side of the bed?"

He'd woken up from an excellent night's sleep after a day spent with Remy. "Maybe."

"Well, I like it. Good to see you happy. Not to mention how handsome you look when you smile." She chucked him playfully on the chin. "What a waste on

that last show you were on." She shook her head with
exaggerated sadness.

Ash snorted. He'd loved playing Zvi, but it was a
relief to play a character who smiled now and again. He
furrowed his brow and pouted, an anti-smile.

Jasmine pinched his bottom lip. "Sassy." She
patted his cheek. "So, lunchtime?"

"Lunchtime."

They headed to craft services. Ash liked eating
with Jasmine, if only because they tended to grab as
much food as the other—Ash because he had a large
body and extensive cardio routine to fuel, and Jasmine
because she seemed to possess a bottomless pit instead
of a stomach.

Ash went with Thai curry and Jasmine with pizza,
and then they settled at a table. She sipped a Coke and
asked if he'd had a good weekend, and he shrugged and
turned it back on her.

He was busting a gut and she was wrapping up
a story involving her boyfriend, her dog, a "puppy
purse," and a trip to the grocery store which had gone
horribly wrong, when Remy arrived.

He stepped into the room and Ash's gaze drifted
past Jasmine and focused. Only his desire to not be
caught out enabled him to turn away. From the corner
of his eye, though, he watched as Remy filled a plate,
grabbed a drink, and then turned to survey the tables.

Ash repressed the urge to wave him over. But it
turned out unnecessary. Remy came their way.

"Mind if I join?" he asked, lifting his tray.

Ash shrugged and titled his head toward an empty
seat, and Jasmine smiled and waved him into it. "Of
course. You're the monster specialist, right?"

Remy put down his food and sat. "Yeah, that's me. I got my master's in monsters and everything."

Jasmine chuckled. "Cool. I didn't know you could do that."

Remy winked. "Definitely. You can get a graduate degree in all sorts of useless things. The trick is convincing someone to pay for your hard-earned knowledge after the fact." The light tone didn't quite hide his self-deprecation.

Jasmine chuckled and said, "Good thing you found someone who needs to know all the mythical creatures."

"For sure. This job is a dream come true. I'm not sure how I beat all the other applicants, but I'm thankful every day."

Jasmine smiled. "Good boy. All right. I've got to run and make a call before they drag us back to set, so I'm going to leave you boys to entertain yourselves." She stood and gathered her tray. "Pleasure to see you again, Remy. And I'll see you on set," she added to Ash, then leaned down to drop a kiss to the top of his head.

Ash didn't flinch, having learned to roll with Jasmine's tactile nature. "Later," he said, and she winked and walked off.

"She always like that?" Remy wanted to know.

Ash shrugged.

Remy smiled and shook his head ruefully. "Well, she's awesome. Mom would call her a card." Ash raised an eyebrow. "Yeah. Have I mentioned my mom is secretly, like, a hundred? One day I'm actually going to make a game of Who Said It with her and like, Agatha Christie characters. Everyone would lose terribly."

"Ye ken?"

"Yup. Each question would be a fifty-fifty shot. Terrible odds," Remy said congenially and then took a bite of his salad. "I often wonder what her kitchen staff thinks of her."

"Oh. Have you not met them?"

Remy offered a weak smile. "No. Not much crossover between Mom's lives these days. Not much time for trivial things like family. My stepdad probably wouldn't see much of her if he didn't 'work from home' and use the restaurant as his office." He poked his salad. "They met because he's her accountant."

Ash didn't know what to say to that. "Oh."

Remy cleared his throat. "To each their own." He took a bite of salad, and Ash drank some of his water.

"So," Remy said, "I was thinking, maybe this weekend we could go do some sightseeing?" His eyes widened, looking hopeful.

He'd been serious about that trade, then. "Alright." Ash gave a wee self-conscious shrug. He didn't know why Remy had asked him, but now he was grateful that he'd spent the year off after *Restraint* finally exploring the city.

Remy licked his lips. "I was thinking maybe we could check out Granville market or maybe the island?"

They were two of the biggest tourist draws in the city, but Ash wasn't going to argue with Remy. He hadn't been to the island since he last filmed there and the market for even longer. It was one of the few tourist sites he'd seen during his first years in Vancouver.

"Sure." Vancouver Island was probably better kept for another day. Hopefully they'd have shooting days out there at some point, so they wouldn't have to spend most of the weekend traveling to and from. The market was easier done. "The market will be busy on the weekend, but not too bad this time of year."

Remy nodded. "Better than nothing. What's the point of going if there are no tourists?"

Ash's eyes widened. "If you say so." He preferred traveling during the off-season.

"Saturday, then? Early morning?"

"Yeah. Easier to get there by bus than car. I'll take a look at the schedule."

Remy nodded, and his soft smile showed more pleasure than many a blinding grin. Ash's heart thumped. "Perfect." Remy's fringe was loose on his forehead today, sweeping messily across to brush his eyebrows. His eyes sparkled.

Reluctant, Ash shook himself and looked at his watch. "I should get back to set."

"Right. Text me?"

Ash didn't suppress the smile those words evoked. "Yeah." He gathered his tray, gave a small finger wave, and headed out. He couldn't help but give one last look over his shoulder before he exited, and he saw Remy smiling absently at his lunch. Ash's own smile was still in place when he got back to set.

**ASH** groaned and reached out of his nest of blankets to silence his alarm.

Waking up early on a day off to catch a morning bus to Granville had seemed like a good idea several days ago, before he did a full-day shoot that hadn't ended until after one.

He groaned again. He'd barely noticed the late hour the night before, when he was working. Michael was a riot, and their on-screen chemistry was undeniable. The current episode had loads of sexual tension for their characters, and Michael always managed to make those scenes the most fun instead of the most awkward.

Now, though, as Ash tried to pull himself from his bed, he was keenly aware that he was closer to thirty than twenty. He had never been good at forgoing sleep, but he'd been able to *survive* it.

*I'm going to see Remy.*

His heart pounded and he got out of bed.

Forty-five minutes later, showered, dressed, and fed, Ash made his way out of the flat and into the surprisingly sunny weather. Hopefully May would bring more such days and chase away the coastal rains.

Remy stood waiting for him at the bus stop. His bright eyes crinkled with delight, and he fair glowed in the sunlight.

Ash shook away his soppy thoughts. "Hallo."

"Hey. Perfect timing. Bus is almost here." He waggled his phone, screen out, so Ash could see the transit app with the GPS feeds.

"Good."

"How's work going? You're filming the episode with Baba Yaga next, right?" He bounced on his toes.

"Yeah. Did you—"

"Consult on it? Yes, I did. I officially helped craft a character." He beamed. "I'm super excited to be able to say that."

Ash smiled, his urge to yawn gone. "I bet."

The bus pulled up and they got on. "How far do we go?"

Ash shrugged. "Couple of stops."

Remy settled in his seat with a little butt wiggle.

"They got you researching anything else?"

Remy grinned. "Yup! They've actually asked me to find a few monsters—gave me some criteria and asked for stuff that might fit." His knee bounced. "They even asked me to throw out some ideas for a werewolf-themed story."

"Oh, fantastic."

Remy nodded. "Yeah. I mean, no guarantees. Maybe all my ideas will be terrible, but it's still cool they asked." His smile morphed into a brave-face type.

"I'm sure they won't be terrible," Ash said. With his imagination and background, Remy would turn out something great.

"Gee, thanks," Remy laughed. "I've always aspired to not terrible." His tone had a hint of sarcasm, but his eyes held warmth.

Ash knocked their shoulders together. "No problem."

When they pulled into the Olympic Village station, Remy arched an eyebrow. "They still call it that?" he asked as they got off the bus to transfer.

"Yeah." Ash cleared his throat. "I got here right after the Olympics. Not sure what it was before."

Remy tilted his head and considered Ash for a long moment. "You must really like it here."

"Yeah." Ash swallowed. "It's home now." Part of him would always miss Scotland, but he couldn't imagine moving back. He'd never really fit in, not like he did here. Besides, Etta wouldn't go for it.

"Well, if you were gonna settle anywhere, I can see here. It's a beautiful city." Remy sighed. "Though I could do with cheaper rent."

Ash snorted. He'd met more than one new costar who'd objected to the cost of housing, and he was grateful he'd been able to buy his place outright. His maw would probably be pleased to know Da's accident had secured Ash some stability at least.

They boarded the second bus and rode it to the base of the bridge. Once there, they walked to the "island" via the small strip of land that connected it to the mainland. The five-minute trek took them down some unassuming brick paths between towering flat complexes and trees, over a small footpath bridge, down another urban path, and out, at last, into Granville.

The island's small community was committed to its trade. As they made their way to the Public Market, they walked past several shops and car parks. It was the land of tourism, and if Remy weren't so intent upon his goal, he would have taken them off course several times over, judging by the cooing and intrigued noises he made at several storefronts.

"We can investigate them later," Ash suggested, and Remy beamed at him.

When they finally arrived and wandered through the halls of the Granville Island Public Market, Remy moaned in delight over the displays of food, each laid out to their best drool-worthy advantage.

Remy bought a blueberry-lemon oat scone and Ash a cornbread muffin, and then they both got drinks. Ash conceded to Remy's bullying to forgo his usual tea and begrudgingly purchased a decadent vanilla latte, and they settled in one of the small-business cafés to drink locally roasted brews while they marveled over their breakfast treats. Well, Remy did. Ash spent more time taking in the sight of Remy's lashes fluttering when he sipped his coffee or took a bite of scone, and the sound of his indecent moans as he savored each bite. Ash had never seen anyone enjoy food so much—well, except for Remy himself when they met. Though Ash didn't remember Remy being so... suggestive back then.

Ash shifted in his seat and hoped Remy didn't notice.

He had barely touched his muffin by the time Remy brushed off his fingers and asked if Ash enjoyed his breakfast. He eyed the treat, so Ash pulled it closer and pointedly tore off a bite.

As Ash ate, Remy rambled on about the people walking past and about seeing if there was a local ice-hockey beer league worth joining, and spun the idea of walking dogs here for cash to "keep my hand in, and also maybe to learn about the city a bit more."

Once Ash had finished eating, they picked up their coffees and wandered about again. Seeing as they weren't yet ready to buy their lunch and there was a limit to how much drooling Remy could do over the edible displays, Ash suggested they go for a walk.

They meandered about, into the Net Loft and the Creekhouse and whichever other store took Remy's fancy. He bounced with delight over the shops and stalls manned by local artists, spent a great deal of time hemming and hawing over each one, peered closely at paintings and photographs, touched all the jewelry and sculptures, and fondled scarves and fabrics. He was especially fond of holding up accessories and clothing to his body and asking, "What do you think?"

At noon, they wandered back toward the food at the Public Market and picked up some brie and garlic salami and a black-olive loaf. Remy made cooing noises over the side dishes in the cheese shop, so Ash picked up some apricots and toasted nuts too. Then they headed outside and settled down to a picnic. Once again Remy moaned his way through the meal and Ash shifted uncomfortably, resigned to his awkward-arousal fate.

"Damn, why is all the food here so good?" Remy asked.

Ash shrugged. "Competition and lots of it."

"Probably." With a chunk of bread, Remy scooped up another bite of brie. "Shame not to have gotten any of the seafood, though."

"We can get some for dinner if you want," Ash said agreeably. He didn't have any other plans, and Etta would be out with her kickboxing buddies that night, so he might as well pick up something here.

"Yeah?" Remy's gaze was warm. "All right. Seafood dinner it is."

And then Ash realized he'd invited Remy over in a rather backhanded manner. *Again*. Abashed, he blushed, looked away, and cleared his throat. "Guid." He ate another bite of bread.

So did Remy.

"I, erm," Ash said, desperate for a distraction, "thought maybe you'd like to go to the children's market." He could already picture Remy running round the toy-filled building.

Remy paused, food halfway to his gaping mouth. "There's a market for children?"

"Yeah. A few blocks away." Ash cleared his throat. "Near where we came in, actually."

"We are so going," Remy gushed.

By the time he bounced gleefully from one store to another in the Kids Market, Ash wondered if he'd made a mistake.

"There's a ball pit! And a candy shop!" He eyed the map on his phone, and Ash pulled him to the nearest storefront.

"What's a Kaboodle?" Remy squinted at the sign and then, with a shrug, skipped off to discover the definition.

The contents of the store—toys—did little to illuminate things, but he didn't seem bothered. He snatched up a Mr. Potato Head and turned it so Ash could see. "Luke Frywalker," he crowed. "And Darth Tater. Oh my God." He swapped out the boxes and peered closely at the contents. "Amazing," he sighed.

*Let me buy it for you.* Ash bit his lip. Remy wouldn't want random presents, especially not from someone he barely knew.

"Oooh, Lego." Remy put down the Potato Head and made for the display. Ash followed. "I had all the Lego as a kid. Loved it, tried to build all the things." He smiled fondly. "What about you?"

Ash shrugged. "More my brother's thing."

Remy shook his head pityingly and asked, "So what was yours?"

Ash felt his cheeks warm. He wondered what Remy would have thought of his collection of My Little Ponies. "I liked Playmobil better." He tilted his head toward their shelves. He could see the cowboy set, his favorite when he was a kid.

Remy smiled and nodded. "Playmobil. Excellent taste." He ran his fingertips contemplatively across the various boxes. "You forget about all of them, you know? All the stuff that made up your childhood, that was so important and you had to have and played with every day, and then suddenly you're doing your best to remember the look or the name of them." Remy touched the box with a construction worker in it. Then he shook himself and smiled winningly at Ash. "What do you suppose is their most annoying toy in here?"

Ash rolled with the abrupt change and took up the challenge. They moved round the displays, looking for noisemakers. Ash found the instruments, and after testing out any that didn't involve putting their mouths where children had presumably put theirs, they agreed the drum was the worst. But Remy wouldn't back down from his stance that the pennywhistle they refused to test would be much more aggravating. They were still bickering about it when they left the store.

"The ball pit!" Remy grabbed Ash's hand and pulled.

"We're not going in there," Ash hastily pointed out, but he didn't drag his feet.

"I know." Remy sighed wistfully. "I don't really want to go in it anyway. I'd probably catch a cold. Still. They're the greatest."

"Not sure I was ever in one," Ash admitted.

Remy made an indignant noise and stumbled to a halt. He whipped round, wide-eyed. "Why would you tell me that when there's nothing I can do to fix it!"

"Sorry." Ash's lips quirked. "I didn't know it would be such a crime." He shrugged—and then noticed their hands were still tangled together. Nervous, suppressing the urge to cast guiltily about, he pulled his hand away and was surprised by a pang of regret.

The market had a sweetie store—because of course it did—and Remy insisted on "sampling their wares," which apparently meant buying several feet of liquorice.

Ash wrinkled his nose. He'd never liked it, but Remy didn't have any such distaste, judging by the way he stuffed the first bite into his mouth and groaned. If there were anything which could convince Ash....

"So good."

Ash cleared his throat. "If you say so."

"Want some? It's really good stuff. Just the right amount of chewy."

Ash shook his head. "Not my thing."

Remy dropped his jaw and gasped with mock outrage. "Are you a liquorice hater? You are, aren't you."

"It's too strong, too bitter."

"What a horrible thing to say!" Remy shook his head. "Well, since you have such bad taste... more for me." He grinned and took another overlarge bite.

He was still munching away when Ash suggested they head home. "We can go back to the market to buy dinner?"

"Yes! Can you believe I haven't had any salmon since I got here? And it's so fresh." He sighed and waved for Ash to lead the way.

They bought a four-pound fillet of salmon and, at Remy's urging, some green beans, scallions, and all the fixings for a Caesar salad.

"Do you have Caesar dressing?" Remy asked as he grabbed the lettuce.

"No?"

"Never mind. I can make some. Just need to grab some anchovy paste. Unless you'd rather vegan? I've got a wicked recipe." He arched his brows, and Ash furrowed his own.

"Whichever you like best."

Remy shook his head. "Let's see if we can find the ingredients here."

They could. Remy found everything he needed as he hopped from one stall to another. He was so busy that he didn't notice when Ash excused himself for a moment and snuck off to another stall.

Once they were laden down with everything Remy needed to make "the best dinner you'll have put in your mouth in ages," they headed for home.

They made their trip in reverse under the still-warm sun, and an hour later, Ash was sat at his bar and watching Remy at work.

He'd offered to help, but Remy shook his head and shooed him away. "I'll work faster this way," he said glibly, then, somewhat ruefully, "Besides, you paid for this dinner, it's the least I can do."

Embarrassed by the gratitude, Ash didn't argue. He didn't wish to draw attention to his more comfortable state, financially speaking. Years earlier, when Ash might have squandered his inheritance—a well-invested legal settlement from his father's accident and the more modest life insurance from his maw's fall to cancer—Langston made sure he couldn't. Ash wasn't rolling in dough these days—this condo had been expensive—but if he were careful, he'd be comfortable for the rest of his life. Which was awkward to tell to someone who probably had student debt and a pittance salary.

So he kept his mouth shut, sat, and watched Remy at work: the captivating and competent way he managed the knife, deftly chopping, and the way he mixed the dressing and cooked the veggies and the fish.

It was like watching a cooking show live. When Remy placed the meal in front of him, Ash lifted his brows and didn't change that assessment. Remy had plated dinner as beautifully as any restaurant-grade chef. Ash narrowed his eyes. "Breakfast wasn't like this," he said softly, without thinking.

Remy laughed. "No." He settled next to Ash at the bar. "But it's possible that tonight I picked some of my most *practiced* recipes." He dimpled at Ash, impish.

Ash looked down at his plate and cleared his throat. "Right. So you cheated."

"I didn't cheat. I put my best foot forward. Now shut up and eat your dinner, you ingrate."

*Ingrate?* Ash mouthed softly, but with a shake of his head, he did as Remy ordered. Oh wow, it were even better than the omelet. Ash hummed in satisfaction and licked his lips. The fish was flaky and buttery on the tongue and counterpointed perfectly with the spicy, garlicky beans and the salty Caesar dressing.

"I need to have you over more," Ash said after a few more bites.

Remy beamed and applied himself to his untouched food. They were quiet but for the sounds of cutlery on porcelain. Remy was probably as hungry as Ash and just as reluctant to waste energy talking.

But once they'd each made a dent, it was easy to resume the conversation from before dinner.

"I'm not saying I don't like him," Remy said again. "He's perfectly fine, and it was great to hear a non-English accent. I'm just saying, I don't like the Capaldi seasons as much as some of the earlier ones."

Ash tilted his head and hid a smile as he wondered if he should relax and concede the argument. He didn't disagree, but he was having fun taunting Remy about disliking the "Scottish" Doctor. "It's the accent, isn' it?" he said, laying his own on thick. "It's no' for everyone. Ye 'hink it's pish."

Remy snorted laughter and squawked about not having it in for the Scots while Ash did his best to keep a straight face.

Ash considered the merits of giving in, but he was having too much fun. "I cannae 'hink another reason to dislike him." He took a pull of his beer. "He's as good a Doctor as the rest."

"It's not him, it's the stories," Remy argued.

"Name a rubbish one, then," Ash challenged.

Remy rolled his eyes. "Where to start? I won't even mention the 'Mr. Sandman' episode"—*Probably for the best, no rebuttal there*, Ash thought as he finished his bottle—"but I've got three words for you: robot Robin Hood."

Ash snorted and beer jumped up his nose. He coughed and wheezed, and dabbed at his face with his napkin. Remy spluttered and clapped a hand to his mouth. It did little to muffle the sound of his laughter, and his eyes danced.

When he finally regained his composure, Ash glared. "I thought you didn't like it because it was 'too dark and melodramatic.' I wasn't expecting you to attack the silliest one."

Remy shrugged, unrepentant. "That episode needs attacking."

Smiling, Ash shook his head and stood. He gathered up their dinner plates and set them by the dishwasher—he'd clean the kitchen later, after Remy had gone—and tossed his bottle into the to-return bin. Then he opened the fridge.

"Ah," Remy sighed knowingly. "I get to see, at last, what you bought so sneakily? And what you tried to hide in the fridge before I saw the box, even though I had to go searching in the fridge for ingredients several times and totally read everything I could on the packaging?"

Ash flushed to have been caught so, but still managed to snort. "You're so ridiculous."

"Yup." Remy smiled innocently. "Now show me me prezzie."

Ash shuddered. "No accents." He pointed a menacing finger.

"I make no promises!"

Ash blew out an exaggerated sigh. He got two forks from the cutlery drawer and debated the merits of plates but decided it would be easier to eat as is.

Then he presented Remy with the treat—a seven-layer cake, each one a color of the rainbow and framed by white icing: Pride Cake.

"Ooh, yay," said Remy. "You didn't."

Ash shrugged. "I saw you eyeing it. And I thought we deserved something for dessert." He handed over one of the forks.

"We have to share?" Remy cast Ash a long, suspicious look and then surveyed the treat as though creating a battle plan.

"Well, I only bought the one. It's rather large." And even though it was Ash's cheat day, they'd already had plenty of carbs and sugar.

Remy attacked first, using the side of the fork to cut off a rather sizable bite of purple and blue.

Ash rolled his eyes and took a smaller bite of red. It seemed Remy was determined to take the lion's share. Not that Ash objected. He liked cake fine—he *was* Scottish after all—but he thought maybe he wouldn't derive nearly as much enjoyment from this treat as he would get from watching Remy eat it. He had closed his eyes and sighed over the first bite, and when he took another, he moaned in delight. Then his eyes fluttered open, and he gave such a warm look that Ash felt it down to his toes. He wanted to look away and mutter, "Welcome," even though Remy hadn't thanked him.

"This cake is *good*."

Ash nodded, mouth dry.

Remy happily took another bite. "Damn. Tell me there's somewhere closer where I can buy this on the regular. No! That's probably a bad idea. I don't need to eat this every day. I'd get fat."

Ash eyed his slim frame. He suspected Remy was the type who wouldn't ever get fat, not even on a diet of cake and more cake. Not like Ash, who was thick through and liable to get thicker if he didn't take care.

He lifted his gaze and it locked with Remy's. Remy lifted an eyebrow and smirked as if to ask, *Like what you see?*

Ash stared back, his own eyebrows lifted in response. He could hardly believe he was—

He ducked his head and forced himself to take another bite. Remy had worked his way through the blue and was making inroads into the green.

"So…. Ah'm no' to tell if the bakery has more locations? Because—"

"No." Remy held up a hand. "I'm sure I'll cave soon enough and look it up and then be disappointed about the results—either because of more or less cake in my future—but until then, I will spend a few weeks in obliviousness." He sighed gustily.

Ash shook his head. "Eat your cake." Then he maybe regretted it when Remy took an extra-large bite.

Alright, he didn't regret it, not when Remy sighed with pleasure. No way Ash could ever regret making him happy.

## Chapter Six

**"YOU** really like him, don't you?" Etta said one evening. She'd been watching silently as Ash did the washing up.

"What?"

Etta shook her head. "Remy. You really like him. You've been smiling nonstop since… well, last weekend."

"Have I?" Ash asked. After their Saturday trip, they met again on Sunday for one of the promised cooking lessons and hid inside during an unending May rain. Ash had much enjoyed watching Remy's biceps in the gray light as he kneaded the from-scratch pasta dough.

"And there was last night," Etta added.

When leaving costume after work, Ash had run into an extra-bubbly Remy, beaming and excited because Janet liked his werewolf ideas so much she'd had a script written. Ash and Remy had gone out for dinner, eating too much sushi and giggling over beers. Ash hadn't floated home until almost midnight.

He'd found Etta on the couch, sleepily watching TV. She denied waiting up for him, but he burned with guilt all the same. She only hummed when he told her where he'd been, but obviously she had more to say now she wasn't half-asleep.

"He's a friend," Ash pointed out.

Etta grunted. "Yes, but…. You *really* like him. I've never seen you like this before." Her head was tilted and she sounded off.

Ash scratched at the side of his nose and pondered her words. "What do you mean, 'like this'?"

She rolled her eyes. "I *mean* it's obvious you're into him."

Ash flushed warm, then cold. "Obvious?" he croaked.

"Well, to me." She shrugged. "I'm not sure anyone else would notice. No one else knows you well enough."

Ash planted a hand on the counter and breathed deeply. He didn't… It was one thing to tell his brother, and another entirely for his friends, acquaintances, *coworkers* to guess.

He didn't want to lose his everything like Sam. A guest star in an early series of *Restraint*, he had *told*. The TV roles had dried up and soon he'd been forced to move back to New York, relegated to the stage, unable to move beyond it, to be a "movie star."

"You're not going to be telling him, then," Etta guessed.

Ash thought about telling Remy that he… liked him. His heart thumped and butterflies filled his stomach. Then reality reasserted. He swallowed and shook his head. *No.*

"Right."

They stood in silence, and Ash did his best to catch his breath.

"You know I'll support you." Etta swallowed. "And if you ever need me to move out—"

"What? No. Of course not." About a year after she moved in, after too much to drink one night, she confessed that all her life she'd thought herself broken for not wanting a happily ever after and had only recently learned she wasn't alone. That night, he made a vow.

"Etta, you will always have a home with me. I'd never kick you out." He swallowed. "And if I ever had a… boyfriend"—though why break an almost-thirty-year streak now?—"they'd know moving in with me meant moving in with you."

She frowned. "Don't be silly. You'd want your own space."

"Have I ever wanted it before?"

She shook her head. "But he—"

"Then he's not worth having."

"Okay," Etta said softly, doubtfully. He wished he could convince her, but nothing short of moving someone else in would prove it.

Which wasn't likely to happen anytime soon, even if Etta side-eyed him a few nights later as he got ready to meet Remy for dinner. He ignored it and left with a quiet goodbye.

**"CUT!"** the director called, and Ash and Michael relaxed out of their staring contest. Michael clapped him on the back and moved off to find his coffee, and Ash ambled over to his director's chair, where Etta was lounging with her phone, one leg hooked over the arm.

"Enjoying the show?"

Etta shrugged. "It's still boring to watch you film," she said glibly. She'd been excited the first time but was no longer impressed by the slow, repetitive process.

Ash rolled his eyes. "Well, you didn't have to come today."

She narrowed hers. "And let you have all the fun? As if." She turned back to her phone and tapped at the screen like Ash didn't know she was playing Candy Crush. Ash's lips quirked in a fond smile, still grateful their friendship hadn't changed any since their talk the week before, even if she still cast Remy suspicious looks every time she caught sight of him.

"How much longer, anyway?" Etta drawled.

"Next scene, I think," Ash said. Etta hummed as if she didn't care.

He grabbed his water and took a deep gulp. Hamish was furious with Niall in this scene, and all the talking had left Ash parched. He was sure he'd already done more talking as Hamish than he'd done in six years as Zvi.

He was putting the bottle back when Remy came tumbling onto the set. "Hi. How's it going so far? Have I missed it?"

"Hello. Good. No." Ash smiled. They'd seen each other the day before, but that didn't stop the happy bubbly feeling in his stomach.

Remy visibly perked up at the last two words and looked around. He swung his arms together, knocked his hands, and swung them apart. "Yay! I didn't want to miss any of it."

"Etta neither."

"Oh, Etta, hi! You don't usually come down to set, do you?" Remy asked apologetically. Ash bit his lip against a laugh.

"No, I don't. I drive him to work a lot, but no point in sticking around. They've got security here." She shrugged. Their bodyguard/client relationship might not be typical, but it worked for them.

"That makes sense. And I don't blame you for wanting to be here today." He bounced on his toes. "To be honest, I kind of came up with the plot just for this."

Ash laughed, unsurprised, and even Etta cracked an amused smile. Remy grinned at them, unrepentant.

A commotion started by the door, and a couple of women walked in. One pulled a wagon with built-up sides.

"Yes!" Remy said and squirmed, clearly curbing the impulse to dash across the room.

Ash bit his lip. "Come on." He gestured to the new arrivals. "They'll want to make sure I'm comfortable with them."

"Yeah?" Remy asked, wide-eyed, and Ash nodded.

When Ash, Remy, and Etta approached the women, who had a bit of a crowd growing around them, Ash could hear whining and yips. Once close enough, he peered into the wagon and found four malamute puppies.

"Oh my God. They are so freaking cute," Remy nearly squealed.

Etta made a soft cooing noise.

Ash introduced himself and his two friends to the ladies. The older one, who had dark curly hair, introduced herself as Rhea and, with a wave to the young blonde with round-framed glasses, added, "This is my assistant, Charlie." Then she turned to the puppies. "And these are Akela, Raksha, Grey, and Leela."

One of the puppies was stood on his hind legs and trying to climb the side, one sat in the corner, watching them all, and the other two moved about, crashing into each other and the first two.

"You should say hello," Rhea said to Ash. He leaned forward and held out his hand. The one on his hind legs stretched for a sniff—then overextended and fell.

Ash and Etta snorted laughter, and Remy squeed.

Chuckling, Rhea reached down, collected the puppy, and after a quick inspection, handed him over to Ash. "You'll probably be working with Raksha a lot. She's the bravest of the bunch."

The gray-and-white puppy squirmed in his arms, climbed his chest, and licked his chin.

"Hello," Ash murmured and stroked her ears. She wriggled some more. "Yer a guid wee pup, aren't you? A terrifying beastie if evah Ah saw one," he continued in an undertone.

Ash heard the sound of a fake shutter and looked up to see Etta smirking behind her phone. She snapped another photo. Ash scowled at her, then glanced at Remy.

His hands were clasped together and held high over his chest, his expression one of pure rapture. "So cute," he sighed with delight.

Ash's stomach flipped. His skin prickled.

Rhea laughed. "You can hold one too, if you'd like."

"Really?" Remy turned his shining heart-eyes to her. Ash looked down at his puppy to hide… whatever it was he felt. Disappointment?

"Of course. Here. Akela's super chill." She picked up the one sat in the corner and handed him over to Remy. He was slightly larger than his sister, with similar gray-and-white markings and a tubbier belly.

Remy cooed at him, rubbed his ears, scratched his chin, and murmured nonsense like "Who's the cutest ickle puppy? Who's the most adorable in the whole world? That's right. You are."

Etta's camera shutter went off again, and Ash wondered if he could get a copy of that picture without Etta taking the piss. Probably not, but it would be worth it.

"I'm so dog deprived," Remy said in a more normal tone but still cuddling the pup close to his chest. "I started dog-walking for cash when I was a kid, so always got doggy playtime, yes I did"—this was said to Akela—"until I moved out here. Maybe I should start up again." He gave a sardonic smile. "Help pay the rent."

Rhea laughed. "You should take my card. I might be able to help with that. In fact I'm sure I could."

Remy beamed at her.

Ash had never before felt so foolish for not owning a dog.

Five minutes later Michael found them each with a puppy in hand and claimed the last one, saying haughtily, "But I'm the *act*or. I'm the one who needs to bond with them, not you." He snuggled Grey close and winked at them.

"Any excuse to be the center of attention or to touch, right?" Ash snarked. He'd been the subject of many hugs, grabs, pokes, shakes, and fist-bumps over the past few weeks. Michael and Jasmine were in fierce competition for most tactile castmate.

Michael glared at him, but considering he had his nose buried in puppy fur, it wasn't very threatening.

That set the tone for the afternoon. Ash and Michael had to curb their desire to simply cuddle the fluffy pups each time the director called action.

The plot was simple: Hamish and Niall, in the middle of a sexual-tension–fueled tiff, find a werewolf puppy during the full moon. As she's fully transformed for the three days, they're unable to find her parents. Cue hijinks as they try to care for a wolf pup.

When Raksha went barreling across the set and ran straight into Ash's shins, he was grateful Hamish's natural inclination was to scoop her up and coo. When the director called cut to reset the scene, Ash turned to find Remy. His expression was soft, and he looked ready to steal the puppy out of his arms. Ash caught his gaze and mouthed *thank you* at him. Then Raksha licked his nose. Remy's face did this sort of meltdown at the sight of so much cute, but he managed a thumbs-up in response to Ash's gratitude.

Despite how boring it was to watch filming, both Etta and Remy lasted through the afternoon, sitting on the sidelines with Rhea and Charlie. Most times when Ash glanced over, their arms were full of napping furball.

When they took a midafternoon break to hydrate all the actors, including the puppies, Remy was stood near Ash's director's chair and grinning so hard his eyes near disappeared.

"Enjoying yourself?" Ash reached for the water bottle hanging off his chair and uncapped it.

"OhmyGod. You have no idea how amazing this is. That's my concept you're filming. My idea, and you're bringing it to life, and I had no idea how amazing it would feel, but it's just so awesome because you're filming *my idea*." Remy pulled in a deep breath.

"So what you're saying is, it's good to see your work being filmed," Ash teased.

Remy punched his shoulder and didn't stop grinning. "Shut up. I've had so many ideas for werewolf scripts after all the research I did into them. Who knew that degree would have any practical use?" His gaze turned to the set and went somewhat distant. Then he refocused on Ash. "Thank you for your part in this."

Ash arched an eyebrow. If Remy thought Ash had pulled strings in any sort of way for him…. Not that Ash wouldn't do it, but he'd never needed to. Remy got here on his own, and Ash had no reason to interfere with that. "This is all on your merits."

Remy pinked a wee bit. "You may not have anything to do with them liking my idea or the writing of the script, but you're helping to bring it all together, and I'm grateful."

"Well. You're welcome, then."

Remy's grin turned back up to full wattage, and he punched Ash's shoulder once again. "Good." Then his gaze softened and his expression turned more serious. "You've helped me a lot in the last few weeks, with making this transition to a new job and city. It's been nice, already having a sort-of friend here."

Uncomfortable, Ash shrugged. He'd never felt very altruistic about "helping" Remy settle in. His motives were pretty selfish. He sighed gustily. "Well, it's been a sacrifice to spend time with you, true, but I pluck through."

Remy chuckled and glared. "Thanks, loser."

Ash was still smiling when they pulled him back on set.

## Chapter Seven

**THREE** days later Remy texted midway through the day to say he was working at home, his roommate was out of town, and maybe Ash would like to come over after work?

So Ash called off Etta and made the trek out to one of the less desirable neighborhoods, to the small two-bedroom walk-up Remy helped rent.

Remy let him in and turned back toward the kitchen. "I'm cooking with Nisha. Find me when you're ready." He grinned and bounded off.

Ash removed his wet jacket and boots, and followed. The space was cramped. As he passed through the living room on the way to the kitchen, he peeked into an open doorway. He recognized the hoodie abandoned on the bed—the Wonder Woman logo discernable despite the crumpled fabric—and frowned with dismay. Remy's bedroom was a closet with ambitions.

Remy stood at the stove, stirring a pot and chatting with Nisha displayed on his propped-up phone.

"I walked a few dogs last week, so that should help. And we'll see about next year." Remy chewed his lip.

Ash frowned. Was Remy having troubles?

"Oh! Ash, come meet Nish." He waved Ash over excitedly. "Ash, Nisha. Nisha, Ash."

Her smiling face filled the screen. "Hello," she said in a rich alto.

"Hi. Good to finally meet 'Donna.'"

Her dark eyes danced beneath her equally dark fringe. "That's me. Thanks for doing that, by the way. Remy won't share copies of the picture"—she cut him an exasperated look—"so it's not like loads of people have seen you in a wig, but that you didn't hesitate made my day."

Ash blushed and shuffled his feet. "You should no' thank me for no' being a bawheid."

She gave a somewhat sharklike smile. "Good answer. Anyway, boo, I should say good night. Early start in the morning, so I better be off to bed."

"Fine," Remy huffed playfully.

"Ingrate. It was lovely to meet you, Ash." She waved and then cut the connection with one last "Love you."

"She seems lovely," Ash said, wishing he could say more without sounding like he was blowing smoke.

Remy beamed. "She really is."

He plated up the chana masala, spinach, and rice, and they settled at the tiny dining-room table. Ash ate a couple of bites and complimented Remy for making another spectacular meal.

"Thanks." Remy smiled.

They ate in silence for a minute, and then Ash, trying his best to sound casual, asked, "Did I hear you say something about dogs?"

"Yeah. That trainer came through. I have a couple of dog-walking clients." He smiled. "Since I don't really *need* to go down to the studio on most days, just like it better than working here"—he waved a hand to take in the room—"it's easy to find the time."

Ash considered this. "You missed it, aye?"

"Yeah. Dogs are the best. And since I can't afford one, this is a good compromise." He smiled, self-deprecating. "Also, better to be paid to spend time with them, rather than the other way around, right?"

Ash nodded. "True." He took another bite and considered his next words as he chewed. He wished he could simply offer to help, but it wasn't his place. And it was probably unwanted, if Remy's insistence on paying his way whenever they went out said anything. "Well, I'm glad you're doing something you enjoy."

Remy tilted his head. "Thanks. It's... good. I'm not worrying about making the rent or anything, not while I'm working for *Mythfits*, but the future isn't exactly certain. My contract's only for the one season, and a second isn't a lock." He snorted. "Finishing the first isn't even guaranteed." He played with his still-clean knife. "To be honest, I'm not sure what'll happen. I've been keeping an eye on job listings, but nothing definite. The joys of an uncertain future." He looked away and then back. "Enough about this. Tell me how your day went."

Ash did.

Later, after dinner, he tapped his pendant and said softly, "Something will turn up. You're too talented to not land on your feet." Then he gathered up the dishes and carried them into the kitchen. He ignored the way his palms stuck to the cooling ceramic and his heart pounded. He was overreacting to giving a simple compliment.

He set the dishes next to the sink, and Remy came in carrying their mismatched glasses. Ash swiped his so he could refill it.

"Thank you," Remy said and bumped their hips together, leaving a tingling hum behind.

Ash's lips curved. "Welcome." He bumped back.

Remy stepped back and, with a smirk, pulled out his phone. "Cleanup tunes!"

Britney Spears came streaming through the sound system. Soon, Remy danced about the kitchen and put leftovers away as Ash washed dishes.

"Ooh!" he crooned happily when the track changed over to a mid-'90s beat. He shimmied his hips, dried dishes, and hummed off-key.

"Terrible," Ash groaned.

Remy raised his eyebrows and shimmied his hips to Mariah Carey. He waved his tea towel round and danced toward Ash. He threw his hands in the air, the towel hanging from his fingers as he cocked his hips back and forth to the rhythm.

Warmth filled Ash's chest. Laughing and trying not to stare at his hips, he covered Remy's mouth with a soapy hand to shut him up. It worked, for a moment. But then Remy pulled away to sing along. "Always be my baby!"

So Ash splashed him with soapy water, and Remy shrieked and danced out of range.

"Mariah hater!"

"I've nothing against her," Ash protested. "She can sing."

"Ouch!" Remy clutched his heart like a drama queen, but before Ash could do more than roll his eyes, Remy recovered. He flipped the tea towel out, looped it round Ash's neck, and pulled him in close as he sang badly. He fluttered his eyelashes, starlet style.

Ash stared down into those brilliant eyes. His gaze flickered to Remy's pouting mouth, and he became suddenly and totally aware of how close they were. Remy's forearms rested against his chest, his toes bumped against Ash's. If he leaned a bit closer, their entire bodies would touch. Ash's skin tingled and he tensed. He couldn't take his eyes off Remy's mouth.

Remy trailed off, and Ash glanced up from his mouth and found Remy staring back at him, wide-eyed. Then Remy flicked his gaze down too and licked his lips.

Oh. Ash had hoped that Remy... but he hadn't—

"Ash," Remy breathed, his body so tense it nearly trembled, "tell me—I mean, I think you—sometimes the way you look at me makes me think you do." He searched Ash's eyes, his lips parted.

Ash stared back, and Remy tilted up, dropped the tea towel, and pressed his hand to Ash's chest. His own right hand gripping the edge of the sink, Ash leaned in.

Remy's lips were soft, faintly chapped, and fit perfectly beneath Ash's own. He gently brushed their mouths together, testing. His skin prickled under Remy's breath.

Ash hesitated. Nerves bubbled in his belly, as he was suddenly, keenly aware of his lack of experience. Off camera, he hadn't kissed anyone in years, too frightened to admit who he really wanted. What should he do? How.... Real kissing wasn't the same as on-screen kissing, surely. Then Remy sighed, parted his lips lightly, and pressed his mouth firmly to Ash's, and all thoughts but the taste and feel of Remy fled Ash's mind.

Remy slid his hands up Ash's chest to cup gently around his face, and Ash fluttered his left hand uselessly before settling it on Remy's waist.

The kiss was almost embarrassingly chaste, Ash thought giddily, a lightness filling his limbs, but when Remy pulled back a few scant inches to look him in the eye, his cheeks were bright red and his eyes dark.

"Please," Remy whispered, his voice husky, "tell me you've been feeling this too. Because I like you, kind of a lot. I'm stupidly gone on your *Doctor Who*- and cooking-show-obsessed self, you nerd, and I thought maybe—"

"Aye," Ash said, fast but unashamed. He swallowed hard, his hands clenched.

"Aye?"

"I do… like you. Er, rather a lot."

Remy's face lit up. "Good." He licked his lips and pushed up onto his toes; their noses bumped together. Giddy, Ash breathed a laugh, and Remy returned it. For a second, they stood so close, sharing breath and smiling at each other like numpties. Then Remy closed the distance and brushed his lips against Ash's mouth again.

Ash at last released the sink and wrapped both hands around Remy's waist. Remy snaked his tongue out and gently licked Ash's lips. Ash let him in, and they kissed long and slow for several minutes, standing in Remy's tiny kitchen, snogging like kids.

Until Mel B broke in suddenly and loudly to demand what they wanted. Remy broke away, laughing. Smiling with all the joy that also filled Ash's chest, he stepped away to dance around and sing "Wannabe."

And Ash, heart pumping, joined him. Laughing and dancing, he curbed the urge to kiss Remy once again. There would be time enough for more of that later.

**THE** following week, one of the more difficult directors decided a scene needed rewriting the morning of the shoot.

Which meant more "hurry up and wait" than usual and plenty of time for Ash to linger on memories of Remy in his arms. Ash sat lounging in his director's chair, thinking about Remy—the taste of his lips, the feel of his body curled against his own—and waiting for orders when Michael found him and slumped into the seat next to him with a sigh.

"Have you heard?"

"No?" Ash tilted his head.

Michael loudly blew out a deep breath. "I guess the douchebag corner of the internet found out about us."

Ash furrowed his brow. "But we're not aired yet."

"No. But some folks have seen the pilot, and the network is already teasing us—premiere next week. So eejits have opinions." He leaned back, settling in.

Ash chewed his lip. "What kinds?" Maybe it was stupid to ask, but he needed to be sure.

"Oh, the usual. We're gross and godless." Ash's stomach dropped. A cloud passed over Michael's expression. "Extra so because me." He waved a hand before his face.

Ash winced. "I'm sorry."

Michael waved him off. "Not you, mate." He sighed.

"No. I guess it just proves we're doing good here, aye?"

Michael nodded. "Definitely. And fuck 'em. Once we're on air, we'll have so many fans they'll drown out the biggotty whinin'."

Ash barked a surprised laugh. "Yeah. We will."

"Damn right! We won't be able to hear them over all the praise." He winked.

"Yeah. Sounds like a plan." Ash did his best to smile and ignore the doubt.

"Anyway, darlin', tell me something nice." Michael rested his head on Ash's shoulder and fluttered his lashes.

An image of Remy with lowered eyelids and a wet mouth, staring at Ash with joy and desire, flashed into his mind. Hoping he wasn't blushing, he pushed the image away and snorted. "It's almost lunch?"

Michael gasped. "Love, you're right. Let's go." He bounded to his feet, grabbed Ash's hand, and pulled a laughing Ash to craft services.

They found Jasmine, Kim, and Remy already seated.

Ash couldn't imagine a better group of costars. He'd been a guest on sets where the actors hadn't got on—had experienced it himself with some of the regulars on *Restraint*—but *Mythfits* had no such tension. Ash and his four costars often found one another during breaks, and lately Remy had sought them out, first shyly and then with increasing confidence when he was routinely welcomed.

"What time on Saturday?" Kim asked in her usual even tone.

Jasmine shrugged. "Anytime after four. I'm not planning on showering until after brunch at noon."

"Isn't that lunch?" Michael cocked his head.

"Not if it's mostly eggs and waffles," Jasmine said loftily. "Anyway, whenever. And bring whatever you want." She smiled at Remy. "Feel free to come along. Kim's bringing her brother, Ash better bring Etta. It's nothing fancy, a casual dinner, might play some games." She pointed a finger in his face. "But no admittance without food." She winked.

"Sounds like fun." Remy smiled—though not the one he'd offered Ash minutes before, Ash noted, butterflies in his belly. "What's the occasion?"

His costars gave Remy looks so incredulous that Ash nearly choked on his salad.

"Watch party," Jasmine said.

"Our premiere," Michael added more helpfully. "We're gathering at Jasmine's to watch together."

"Ooh." Remy sat up straighter. "Well, I'm definitely in for that."

Kim snorted. "Misery loves company."

Jasmine and Michael both aimed a punch to her shoulders.

"Shut up. It'll be great."

"Yeah, sunshine, they'll love us. Me and Ash are irresistible." Michael winked.

Ash shook his head and cast a commiserating look Remy's way—his lips were pressed together and twitched with suppressed laughter. Underneath the table, he pressed his foot to Ash's be-Chucked one.

Warmth burbled in Ash's stomach. This was everything he wanted. He wished to stay in this moment, for *Mythfits* to go on forever. He didnae ken how he'd adjust if he lost *any* of it.


**TIRED,** Ash turned to the lift instead of the stairs and enjoyed the wee rest on the short trip. Halfway through filming a scene, director Bob had decided it wasn't working and ordered they reset, reblock, and restart—hours of work down the drain, and hours of waiting for the new set, which left them hopelessly behind schedule. Bob promised it would be worth the trouble, but as Ash stumbled toward his door after eight, rubbing at his face, he nearly doubted it.

He certainly couldn't thank Bob for ruining his evening plans.

He found the flat quiet but not uninhabited. Etta was curled up in one of the comfy chairs, reading, and Remy sat at the dining-room table, notebooks, laptop, and books laid out before him. While Etta looked serene and comfortable curled up in joggers, Remy was her opposite. His hair was in disarray, his leg bounced, and he scowled at his work.

Ash's heart skipped a beat and then another. For a long moment, he stood and stared, taking in the beautiful face. He and Remy had made plans to cook dinner, and Ash, thinking the delay would be short, told Remy to come over anyway, that Etta would let him in. At least Remy hadn't been forced to twiddle his thumbs while he waited.

Etta looked up when Ash shut the door. She glanced at Remy, then back at Ash, raised her eyebrows, nodded at his frustrated… friend, and turned pointedly back to her book. Blushing, recalling the way Etta waggled her eyebrows when he told her about the kiss, Ash shook his head, slipped off his Blundstones, and walked over to the oblivious Remy.

Ash had conjured so many plans for that evening— most of which involved the couch and the continued exploration of Remy's body as Remy showed Ash how to kiss and cuddle—but the weariness in his body and the wrinkle on Remy's forehead said those plans were lost.

"Hey," Ash said quietly, but Remy still jumped.

"Oh! When did you get in?" Remy blinked up at him a few times, his brow furrowed.

"Just now. You doing alright?"

Remy turned back to his laptop, and the lines between his eyes grew deeper. "Yeah...." He chewed his lip. Ash pulled out the chair next to him and sat down. "Janet... suggested I give her a script if I wanted to, write up one of the ideas I've given." He stared at his computer, refusing to meet Ash's gaze. "But it's not... it's not working. It's—the characters are flat, and the plot doesn't make sense, and I can't get the two main parts to marry together, and—" He took a shuddering breath. His mouth curved downward as he scanned the screen. Ash wanted to hug him. Could he? Was that allowed now?

He tilted his head and kept his hands to himself. "So you have writer's block. Maybe if you left it alone tonight—"

"But it's not just tonight," Remy snapped. Then his shoulders slumped and he rubbed at his face. "Sorry. I'm frustrated, it's been a week of tortured writing, but you didn't deserve that."

Ash shrugged. "I can take it. But is there something else the matter?"

Remy turned to him, cocked his head, and stared. Then he sighed. "Insightful. I guess it feels like a job interview. I'm just an intern right now, which pays... okay, but if I can prove to Janet that I can write, then maybe I'll be able to get myself a job as a writer next year—if not on *Mythfits*, then on another project. Janet has connections."

Ash swallowed. "Oh."

"Yeah." Remy rubbed his face again. Since when did he have bags under his eyes?

Ash pushed away thoughts of Remy leaving for another show, and focused on what was important. "Well, maybe this is a very important script, and maybe it's giving you troubles, but I think it's late enough tonight to put it aside." He reached out and flipped the notebook closed. When Remy didn't object, he moved in for the laptop. Remy sighed and didn't protest that either. "And maybe, if you can, you should stop putting so much pressure on this one script."

Remy huffed. "Nisha said the same thing, but I don't know how."

"Well. You won't solve it tonight. But maybe, tomorrow, if you like, I could help?"

Remy eyed him suspiciously. "How?"

"I don't know. Maybe read what you've got?" Remy's eyes widened with such clear horror Ash added, "Or you could bounce ideas off me? Sometimes saying something out loud...."

"Maybe," Remy conceded. "You're definitely right about it being quitting time." He stood. "There's leftover dinner if you want some."

Ash nodded. He settled at the breakfast bar and watched Remy plate him a dish of leftover lasagna and heat it up.

Etta closed her book and approached the kitchen. "I'm off to bed." She ruffled Ash's hair and waved at Remy. "Night."

It was early for bed, but Ash wouldn't point that out. He nodded his thanks.

"Night."

Remy pulled the lasagna from the microwave and placed it in front of Ash, then took the seat next to him.

After a few bites, Ash smiled at him. "This is good. Thank you. For coming over and for making me dinner even though—" Remy waved him off. "Well. Glad you're here."

"Me too," Remy said with a tiny private smile.

"Good."

"And I'm sorry for—no, listen. I'm sorry I'm in a mood, but please know it has nothing to do with you. You are the only good thing about this stupid week—I know it's only Wednesday—but I need you to know that you are a very, very good thing." His voice dropped and his eyes turned warm.

After a moment's hesitation, Ash leaned in and pressed a kiss to Remy's cheek. Remy turned and brushed their lips together. The kiss was soft and slow and tasted of lasagna. Ash pulled reluctantly away and turned back to his dinner, too famished not to, and they sat in comfortable silence. Though Remy skootched closer to press their shoulders together.

After Ash was fed, they settled on the couch for a time, pressed close together, kissing like teenagers, touching above the belt, sliding their lips slowly, almost sleepily together.

Later, as Ash watched Remy get into a cab—which he had ordered and paid for over Remy's protests—and drive away, he couldn't think of anything he'd rather be doing.

**THE** following afternoon Etta and Ash walked to Jasmine's, Ash carrying the bag with drinks, Etta the salads.

They arrived to find Remy sitting at Jasmine's breakfast nook and chatting with her and her boyfriend, Amal.

"Hey! Drinks in the fridge."

"Hi," Remy said, looking relieved to see them.

Jasmine laughed. "Next time I invite someone new over, remind me to explain about time. Poor guy has been here thirty minutes with nothing to do but watch Amal and me cook."

"And cuddle the dog," Remy said, with a gesture to the furry mop in his lap. Pickles had flopped, leaning heavily into Remy's stomach and looking supremely pleased. It turned out to be true love, Ash guessed, because Pickles spent most of the evening following Remy around and asking for more cuddles. Ash tried not to be jealous of a dog and was successful—some of the time.

The group filled out, and once Kim arrived with her brother, Jordan, in tow, their party was complete. They loaded up the coffee table in the living room with the food and settled round it. Observing the limited number of seats, Remy shrugged and sank to the floor, rested his back against the frame of the couch, and bumped his shoulder into Ash's knees, making them tingle at every accidental brush. Ash longed to tangle his fingers in Remy's hair, so he curled them to avoid temptation.

And he only side-eyed Pickles a little when she curled into Remy's lap.

Jasmine pulled out 90's Trivial Pursuit. "Stuff it, Amal," she said preemptively, smiling. "We can't play a game where we have to hold stuff, our hands are full of food."

"And beer," Miya pointed out. She was curled up in a wingback, with her plate on her knees and a bottle of stout in her left hand.

They broke into two teams, and the battle began. It became rapidly apparent that any game involving Remy and Jasmine would be played to win. While everyone else seemed willing to be lenient—surely a last name was sufficient?—Jasmine gave no quarter. Remy sat up and leaned into the board. "Right," he muttered to himself, with a gleam in his eye that made Ash want to snog him, and then proceeded to destroy them all with his pop-culture knowledge.

"You're a baby. How do you even know *Growing Pains* existed?" Jasmine moaned, exasperated.

Remy smirked and slotted the pie piece into the token. "I have my ways."

"Seriously, though, you can tell us, your teammates," Miya said.

Remy considered this. "Good point. I was an only child with access to a lot of reruns." He smirked, and Ash wished he could kiss him.

Jasmine groaned and grumbled, and Remy picked up the die to roll it again.

Fortunately for everyone else, the battle royale across the coffee table was called to a halt at five to seven.

Jasmine cleaned up the board, muttering darkly about ringers, while Amal, shaking with laughter, turned on the television.

The room buzzed with anticipation. Everyone but Kim and Amal had already seen the pilot. They knew it was good, but soon they'd be able to check Twitter and see what *people* thought. And according to Janet, they expected a lot of people to tune in, what with all the drama already on the internet.

They made a pact to keep their phones tucked away for the duration, and they all sat on their hands, even through the too-long advert breaks.

But as the credits finally rolled, and the two new viewers began to heap praises upon the rest of them, Remy, Michael, and Jasmine whipped out their phones.

Ash touched his coin. His stomach clenched. He might be sick.

Jasmine crowed. "They fucking love us!"

"Yeah?" Miya asked in a tiny voice.

"Feck yeah!" Michael agreed. "Love. Us." He scrolled frantically.

Ash thought he might faint with relief.

Jasmine squirmed with delight. "I keep seeing hashtag representation matters." She looked up to give them all a sunny if slightly watery grin.

"Good," Kim said fiercely.

Remy nodded. "Damn, I can't even—there's so much good and for every one of you. People are super stoked about the show." He frowned. "Well, except for the douchebags, but the positives are definitely outweighing the negatives." He shot a smile at Ash, who wished he could lean in and kiss it. He pressed his knee to Remy's shoulder instead. For a second Remy's eyes seemed to smolder at him. *Later*, they promised. Then he turned back. "They love you."

Grinning, Michael agreed. "They've dubbed us Niamish." He looked at Ash. "Told you they'd love us, darlin'."

Despite himself, Ash's cheeks flushed hot. He could hardly believe people supported this—*him*. "Of course they do," he managed. "I'm charming."

Michael cackled and went back to reading tweets. "I'm scrolling the Niamish hashtag, which is surprisingly busy already. They think we're adorable." He paused. "Oh my." He fanned himself with an empty hand. "This

one does not think we're 'adorable.'" He winked. Ash
would have blushed again, were he able.

"Ladies and gentlemen," Jasmine said imperiously,
holding up her beer, "I think we can call our premiere
a success."

"To us!" Michael cheered.

And they all answered in kind: "To us!"

Ash sipped his beer and, despite his burning desire,
didn't take Remy's hand or kiss his smiling mouth.

## *Chapter Eight*

**THE** large beast came barreling out of the woods, crashing through the underbrush, swept a branch to the side, and roared.

Of course, without the animal noise which would be overlaid during postproduction, the roar sounded rather human and weak, but Ash could imagine the effect that could be created with close-up shots, mood lighting, and a large predator's snarl.

*Mythfits* wouldn't do that. Well, they would, but then they would also cut to Ash and Miya cooing over the sight of a sasquatch in the wild. Apparently brownies and weather spirits weren't frightened by seven-foot-tall man-apes protecting their territory.

Martin, the guy in the costume, motioned for a bottle of water. There were two versions of the mask, one he could talk in and one he couldn't. He was wearing the second now, as it was easier to put on and they were only filming action shots—it was highly entertaining to watch a sasquatch drink through a bendy straw.

"All right, let's get set up for the first interactions," the second director, Sabina, said. "We'll run through the entrance again, but this time let's swivel round to see Hamish and Nariko unflinching, despite the bigfoot in their face."

Ash looked at the rig and figured it would take less than an hour to refigure everything and be ready for shooting. He picked up *Boy Erased* and settled into his chair to read. Then he pulled out his phone to check it and smiled when he saw the message from Remy.

*So bummed I wasn't deemed crucial for island shooting D: why @ universe!*

Smiling, Ash tapped out a quick reply. *You're not missing much. Mostly trees and cameramen.*

*Not helping! I looked at pictures of the island's national parks. Jealous forever.*

It was indeed unfortunate. But the cost of getting him to Vancouver Island and putting him up was prohibitive when he could advise and script-doctor over the phone—even if Remy would love it here.

Unless….

There was no reason Remy couldn't come anyway. They both had the weekend off, miraculously, and Ash was already here….

Thanking the universe for mobiles and data, Ash phoned the Empress and inquired about a room. Why yes, they did have one available for the weekend. A view of the harbor? Not a problem. Two beds? Well, no, sir, but they could give him a suite with a king and a pullout sofa. For Friday and Saturday night? Perfect.

Once the reservation was made, he switched back to the text thread with Remy.

*I'm languishing in the office with no one else around, revising another script and waiting by the phone in case someone calls. And thinking about your face and your lips and your beard.*

*I'm so bored.*

*Did you go back to filming? Because ugh if you did. I need you to entertain me.*

Flushing at the memory of Remy's pink cheeks, Ash shook his head. *Not filming, on the phone. Wanted to be sure was possible before told you. Want to take ferry to Victoria on Friday and spend weekend here? Can go back to mainland Sunday.*

*WHAT?!!!!! Not serious!* was the instant reply. Followed by, *Serious?*

Chuckling, Ash wrote, *Of course serious. Come. I'll show you around.*

There was a long pause. Ash waited and waited, his book long forgotten. But there was still no answer when the director called to him a minute later.

Scowling, Ash set his phone aside. He went to work and pushed his anxiousness down, and doing his best to ignore it.

Fortunately Hamish was an especially confident creature, comfortable in his skin and not prone to worry. The only wrinkle in his life was Niall, who wasn't in the scene, so Hamish hummed placidly under Ash's skin.

Playing him was better than therapy.

An hour later Ash was finally able to check his phone. Remy had sent two messages, twenty minutes apart.

*I would love to but can't. No way I can afford.*

*Sorry :(*

Ash frowned at his phone and wrote as quick as he could, *Don't be silly. Weekend is on me. My treat. Will only cost you ferry ticket.*

*Dude! I couldn't!*

*Yes you could.*

*Living in Vancouver is expensive. I can't let you pay for a last minute hotel because of me!*

Ash scowled. He wondered how to get out of this conversation quickly and tactfully, but eventually gave it up for lost *Living here is lot less expensive without rent/mortgage. Let me do this for you?*

Again, the wait was excruciating. He'd never done anything like this before. Maybe it was too soon? He might have crushed his water bottle if it weren't made of metal.

But finally the answer came, simple and such a relief that Ash's heart leapt.

*Okay.*

Ash curbed the desire to fist pump—well, for a moment.

It turned out Hamish's implacable calm was more difficult to harness when Ash's happy heart couldn't stop beating double time.

**REMY** arrived on the island in the late afternoon, well before Ash finished work. He sent more than one apologetic text as the filming dragged on and on, and insisted Remy go to the Empress.

*I know they won't let you in, but wait in the lobby. I'll be there asap.*

ASAP turned out to be almost eight, and Ash felt extremely guilty as he slunk into the historic building…

until he saw Remy, lounging on a leather couch and chatting with three other early-twentysomethings.

Ash licked his lips and walked up to them.

Cuddled close and holding hands, two women sat on the same couch as Remy. One had long, curly hair in an intricate braid, the other a shaved head revealing a tattoo. Their friend was male, dressed in a pink button-down, and had a stylized cut with shaved sides and long fringe. He flicked his head to get the hair out of his eyes, and they widened as he noticed Ash and looked him up and down.

Then Remy saw him, their eyes caught, and a smile lit his face. Ash answered it with a more subdued, shier one. "'Ello."

"Hey! You finally escaped."

"Fin'lly," he agreed. He was knackered, and after a day as Hamish, his accent was slipping. What followed came out very Scottish. "Readay tae check in?"

"Oh my," said the man on the couch. "Damn." He sighed and fanned himself. "Nice meeting you, Remy. But we won't keep you any longer… not that we could." He looked Ash up and down, again, and then sighed, *again*. Ash went red.

Laughing, Remy stood and said goodbye. "Libby, Sarah, Beau, it's been a pleasure."

The one with the braid waved, and a rather sparkly diamond glinted on her left ring finger. "Later. Maybe we'll catch you again. Though, maybe not." She also eyed up Ash, and if he could burn hotter, he would do.

Since reaching adulthood and growing into his ears and weight, Ash had been blatantly admired many times. He didn't think he would ever get used to it, even if he'd learned to ignore it. But never had anyone insinuated he and another man were an item. Butterflies

swooped into his stomach. These strangers thought….
It had been a long time since he'd last dreamed about
others thinking of him as part of a set.

Remy slung his bag over his shoulder and motioned
for Ash to lead him to check-in. "Sorry about that. I
didn't tell them anything, but they assumed and…."

"It's fine," Ash said, surprised to find it was. They
clearly hadn't recognized him. Being seen as gay…
well, it had been a relatively painless experience.

Though probably for the best that Remy hadn't
confirmed anything. Really.


**THE** suite was fancy. It had three rooms—the bedroom,
bathroom, and living room—and all the furniture was
pristine, the pillows perfectly plumped. The hotel
might be a historic monument, but the room had all the
comforts of modern furnishings and décor.

After a brief look round and considering the state
of his boots—dirty after three days filming in a national
park—Ash kicked them off, dropped his bag by the
couch, and went to check out the view. He might be
getting somewhat jaded about such luxuries, because
when he turned back, Remy still stood by the doorway,
his mouth wide enough to catch flies.

"Ash," he said somewhat uncertainly. "How…? This
looks expensive." He turned to Ash, chewing his lip.

Ash shrugged it off. "Not so much."

"But… we could have gone somewhere cheaper."

Ash shook his head. "Naw, the Empress is the
place to stay." Remy didn't look convinced. "I told you,
I can afford it." Ash licked his lips. "And I wanted to do
this for you, to spend time with you."

Remy considered him for a long moment, then gave a hesitant soft smile. "Okay," he murmured.

Ash smiled. Then, because he couldn't deny himself a second longer, he crossed the room to kiss that inviting mouth. "Hey you."

"Hey." Remy pushed up to kiss him back. Warmth spread from his lips and his hands where they touched. Ash wanted to lean into it, into Remy, to learn what came next—

His stomach let out a large rumble, and Remy pulled away with a laugh.

Too tired to do anything else, Ash called down to room service. Before long, a tray arrived, weighed down with hot chocolate, popcorn, ricotta and fruit, and carrot cake.

Ash tipped the lady, then turned back to see Remy already had a spoonful of ricotta in his mouth and was moaning.

"Oh my God. Totally worth staying here for the food," he sighed with delight.

Ash shook his head and, as he settled next to Remy on the couch, lifted a cup of cocoa made with heavy cream and dark chocolate, according to the menu. It was pure decadence. He'd need to wash it down with a ton of water. Worth it, though, after his long day.

"Good?" Remy asked. When Ash nodded, he reached for his own mug and hummed with delight. "I could get used to this," Remy sighed, then snagged a strawberry and ran it through the ricotta.

*Me too*, Ash thought, not thinking of the menu at all.

"Even the popcorn is extra good." Remy almost sounded betrayed, and Ash snickered into his drink.

Buoyed by a full stomach, a few ounces of caffeine, and Remy's presence, Ash pushed aside his

other burning desires—there would be time enough—
and coaxed Remy out for a walk.

Inner Harbour was striking at night. Located inland
and surrounded almost entirely by the city, the port in
Victoria was unusual, Ash suspected, because from
almost every direction, more of Victoria lay across the
ocean waters.

Ash and Remy crossed the street, walked to the
footpaths near the water, and headed north—so Remy
said. They ambled, taking in the sights. Despite the
hour and season, some people lingered, though Ash bet
not nearly as many as there would be in a few weeks
when summer tourism began.

Despite the chill in the air, the evening was
pleasant. Though possibly Ash's perceptions were
colored by the warmth which shot up his arm and
settled in his belly every time Remy's hand bumped
against his. His fingers tingled with the desire to curl
around Remy's. He brushed them together deliberately,
spotted a laughing couple up ahead, then pulled away.

They curved around the bend of the marina and
walked the length of a dock, Remy pointing out the
different ships and sights, and sighing over the view.
The last rays of light were fading from the skies,
glinting off the water, and peeking from behind the
buildings located farther west of them.

"It really is beautiful here. And," he said, "rather
romantic, yeah?"

Ash cleared his throat. "Aye."

Remy smiled—it wasn't his usual bright beaming
grin, but something softer, satisfied. "Yeah. I thought so."

They stood in silence for several long moments,
watching the lights dim. Finally Remy turned with
shining eyes and said, "Should we keep heading north?"

Ash nodded.

They walked back to the main path and continued their tour of the port.

"Have you ever been boating?" Remy asked.

Ash shook his head. "You?"

"No." Remy contemplated one of the many moored crafts.

"Would you like to? We could probably hire someone to take us out, or join a tourist thing...."

Remy shook his head. "I don't think I want to go boating." His eyes sparkled with mischievous suggestion. "I don't want to share you this time."

"Oh." Ash stuffed his hands awkwardly into his pockets.

Their pathway seemed to be converging with a more commercial area, with cars and roads.

"Maybe time to turn around?"

Ash agreed.

The Empress, Ash thought when it came into view, was stunning at night. Many of the buildings on the harbor were lit, but the Empress stood dramatic against the darkening sky and somehow managed to look more old-fashioned, grand, and romantic, despite shining with modern lights.

"Ohh," Remy sighed.

"It's lovely," Ash whispered.

"Very."

Ash turned from the Empress to a no-less-beautiful view of Remy, the lights shining off his green eyes and playing against his skin. No, Remy wasn't *just* as beautiful, but more so. For one wild moment, Ash thought he should definitely kiss him, right here, right now.

Remy turned to him and inhaled sharply. "Ash," he murmured.

Their gazes caught, and Ash couldnae look away. He wasn't sure what, if anything, he should say.

Remy seemed not to have any such doubts. "It's so romantic here. Everything—the hotel, the walk." He turned to look at the Empress once again. "This weekend is so perfect. I can't believe anyone would— did do this for me." He kept his voice low, not that anyone was close enough to overhear.

Ash's palms sweated and his heart pounded and he ached to take Remy into his arms. Once again Remy had spoken his mind and humbled Ash with his bravery. And Ash couldn't help but respect it, to answer it with courage of his own.

"You're worth it. You'll always be worth it."

And there was the blinding grin back again. Remy took a half step forward, and Ash felt himself leaning in, drawn by new memories of that soft, delicious mouth.

Kissing Remy was addicting. The feel of his mouth beneath his own, the taste, the warmth of his lips closing about Ash's—

A bell jangled, and they parted as a bike zoomed past them.

"Jerk," Remy said, but his tone was light and happy.

Ash turned to him, and Remy was still grinning.

"Time to go back to the hotel?"

"Aye," Ash said embarrassingly quick. But Remy seemed rather gratified by it, so Ash didn't waste time on embarrassment. Instead he curled his hand around Remy's, surprised by his boldness, and tugged him in the direction of the hotel.

Ash wondered what Remy expected tonight. They'd kissed several times, but surely he'd want more? They'd not yet talked about things, only snogged like teenagers. Suddenly the hotel room with its one bed seemed very suggestive.

In the lift, Ash took a shaky breath. His skin prickled. He felt all too conscious of Remy next to him, their hands entangled. He clenched his free hand and tried to ignore that awareness and the desire curling in his belly. With Remy vibrating beside him, he felt right, like he was where he should be.

But what if he was wrong? What if Remy wanted more than he could give? Ash had never—

The lift doors opened.

Once in the room, they stared at each other for a long moment. Ash wasn't quite sure what to do next. He wiped trembling hands on his jeans. What should he do? Would they.... What if he was bad at it?

Fortunately Remy didn't lack confidence. He stepped forward and placed his left hand on Ash's chest and settled his right on his cheek. He stroked a thumb across Ash's cheekbone, sending shivers through him.

Ash curled his hands around Remy's hips and brushed his own thumbs along the harsh ridge of them, thrilling at being able to touch. Remy was solid. Ash squeezed to feel the strong bone under his fingers.

Remy lifted and kissed him, sliding his wet mouth against Ash's.

Panting, Ash tightened his hold on Remy's hips and pressed back, enjoying the newly familiar touch.

Remy snaked his left arm around Ash's neck, and Ash wrapped his round Remy and pressed it to the small of his back.

Remy hummed, soft and eager, slipped his tongue out, and ran it along Ash's lower lip.

Ash gasped and then groaned when Remy slid his tongue in. Ash clutched him, tangling his fingers in the cotton of his shirt.

He felt hot. His skin tingled and burned under Remy's touch. Remy rubbed his thumb over Ash's cheekbone again, and a shiver ran down his spine.

He pulled back. "Remy."

Remy shivered in his arms and then purred softly, "Ash, fuck. So good." He bumped their noses together again.

Ash let out a shaky breath. "Yeah?"

"So good." Remy smiled. He licked his lips and then asked, "Wanna go make out on the couch?"

"Aye," Ash breathed out shakily. Memories of other evenings pressed together left him hot and panting.

Remy tangled their fingers and stepped back. Then he pulled Ash across the living room to the sofa.

Ash swallowed hard. He was nervous, excited… afraid.

What if Remy expected….

He couldn't *not* tell, surely. Maybe he should have confessed two weeks ago.

"I've—" He swallowed. Remy watched him with kind eyes, steady, patient, and took Ash's trembling hands in his own. "I've no' slept with someone as *me*." He swallowed and then whispered, "Never with a bloke."

Remy blinked. "Oh. Well, there's no rush. And I'm more than happy to be your first." Remy smiled and placed his hands flat on Ash's chest, gently pushed him back so he sat, then stretched out on the sofa with his shoulders and head on an armrest.

Remy swung a leg over—literally—kneeled on the cushions, and hovered for a long moment. They'd not done this before, one on top of the other. Slowly Remy leaned forward and brushed their mouths together in a long, slow tease of catching, dragging lips, which sent heat rushing through Ash and tingled in his fingertips and toes.

Shaking, Ash wrapped his hands around Remy's hips once again, needing to hold on to something or else he might float away. Or maybe tremble into a million pieces. His mind rushed with a thousand thoughts—Remy wanted to have sex with him, and he was going to sleep with a man, with Remy—and yet it seemed totally incapable of processing anything as Remy parted his lips and pressed himself closer.

He shifted and lay down on top of Ash, their legs tangled together, their chests pressed tight. He threaded his fingers in Ash's hair, and Ash ran his hands up and down Remy's back. He was so solid and warm, and his body weighing Ash down sent a thrill of delight up his spine. He couldn't deny Remy was there, real, and in his arms.

Remy scratched his nails over Ash's scalp, and Ash gasped. *Too much.* He reached up and took Remy's hands in his, a silent request for no more. Remy murmured nonsense into his lips, then pressed their hands down onto the couch and squeezed, a silent *I hear you.*

Time slipped away as they touched and explored, but when Remy sneaked his hands toward Ash's belt, he stiffened. His brain screeched to a halt.

Remy pulled back, slid his hands up to Ash's chest, and whispered, "We should probably go to sleep."

"Probably," Ash agreed, near choked by gratitude, and tightened his arms.

Remy laughed, kissed him again, then pulled back. "Come on. Let's go cuddle in the bed."

Once up, they brushed their teeth, changed into pajamas—in separate rooms—and then curled up together under the comforter, limbs entwined. They weren't using much of the king-sized bed.

They snogged again.

"This is good. Perfect," Remy said softly.

Ash hummed his agreement and pressed a soft kiss to Remy's nose.

It didn't take long for them to drift to sleep, still curled up together, sharing space, their fingers intertwined.

## *Chapter Nine*

**CURLED** on his side and cramped on the edge of the mattress, Ash woke up and stared at Remy splayed out on his back, his legs akimbo. His right arm was reached toward Ash, and his left flung over his head. Ash studied him.

With the early morning light casting shadows and making the sweep of his lashes appear longer, Remy looked angelic, sweet, nothing like the violent danger he embodied while they slept. Ash had woken suddenly in the middle of the night after Remy struck him in the face. Ruefully, he rubbed a hand over his cheek and wondered if Remy would always be a danger to sleep with. Giddiness bubbled in him. He should soon find out firsthand.

Ash had acted the morning after a time or two on-screen, but had never lived it. The one time he slept with a woman had been about "having fun" at uni—or trying to—not romance, and they'd awkwardly parted ways before they fell asleep.

Waking up with Remy was nothing like TV. For one, Remy didn't wake up shortly after, catch Ash staring, and smile. Instead, Ash got out of bed, brushed his teeth, called for breakfast, and after a long moment's deliberation, settled on the couch with his book. He was still there when room service arrived.

It was possible he'd gone a wee bit overboard. But not knowing what Remy might want, he ordered some of everything—waffles with fruit, banana-bread french toast, a garden-veggie omelet, a simpler eggs-and-bacon dish, as well as muffins and croissants, and coffee, tea, and juice.

Definitely overboard.

Figuring leftovers never hurt anyone, Ash shrugged and considered the next issue—if Remy didn't wake soon, breakfast would go cold.

He chewed on his lip and was still considering the issue when Remy stumbled out of the bedroom, rubbing at his hair, flannel trousers slung temptingly low on his hips.

"Morning," Remy said around a yawn. "Do I smell bacon? And coffee?" He blinked at Ash, kissed his cheek, then noticed the breakfast. "Oh, you sweet man, you. You're perfect." He pressed a lingering kiss to Ash's mouth, dragging his lips and swiping at Ash's with his tongue. Then he pulled back and snagged a piece of bacon, leaving Ash hot and bothered in his wake. He took a bite and then stuffed the end into his mouth to hold it as he poured himself a cup of coffee.

He ate the rest of the bacon and doctored the cup, then sat down and cradled it to him.

Bemused, Ash settled across from him and poured some tea.

"I used to hate coffee," Remy said after a couple of minutes of silence. Ash looked up from his waffle. "Hmm, very proud of not liking it too. *I* couldn't bear it without plenty of cream and sugar, much too bitter." He sighed. "Then I went to grad school and got hopelessly addicted." He yawned, scratched his nose, and then seemed to take in the spread at last. He stared at it for a moment, blinking, then shook himself. He observed the contents with narrowed eyes, a general surveying the battlefield. Then he reached for the french toast and placed a slice on an empty plate. "Thanks for breakfast."

Ash shrugged. "No problem." He'd been prepared to feel awkward. Leave it to Remy to know what to do.

Remy took a couple of bites, drank more of his coffee, and at last seemed to wake up. "Oh man. Sorry. I'm kind of useless in the morning." He cocked his head. "How are you? Did you sleep okay? And thanks for all this. It's amazing, and I would have been way too useless to order any of it." He smiled, the soft one Ash was fast becoming addicted to.

Uncomfortable with the gratitude, Ash said, "I slept alright." Then, eyeing Remy from beneath his lashes, he added slyly, "Well, except for the attack."

Eyes narrowed, Remy asked, "Attack?"

Ash nodded. "Aye. In the wee hours. Me, I was having a good dream when someone decided to wallop me in the face." He smiled to show he was uninjured.

"Well," Remy said, gaze still shrewd, "maybe you deserved it."

"While I was sleeping?"

"Hmm. You said you were having a good dream. Maybe someone was trying to ward off your amorous advances?"

Ash snorted. *Amorous?* "If I had any, I doubt anyone here would object to them." He gave a defiant stare, which Remy met, eyes still slitted.

The contest lasted for half a minute before Remy broke. He chuckled and said, "Oh man, you're probably right. Probably would have sleepwalked my way through the make out." His gaze turned searching as he swept it over Ash's face. "Did I really hit you in the face?"

Ash shrugged. "Aye. No' very hard, though. I survived." He took a sip of juice. He meant to leave it there but suddenly felt compelled to blurt out apologetically, "But I might have escaped to the other end of the bed."

Remy laughed, sounding relieved. "Oh, good!" He shook his head. "I've been told I'm terrible to sleep with. I once literally kicked my first boyfriend out of bed." He grinned sheepishly, and the knotted tension Ash hadn't known was building began to loosen.

"Really?"

"Yeah. We were in the dorms, small beds. Poor guy. He cursed me out—in two languages, no less, French and English. I'm a pretty heavy sleeper, but that woke me up. Well, him and his roommate, who also felt the need to swear at me." Remy grinned, looking unrepentant.

"So, you're saying I should be grateful the bed was too large for you to throw me out of it?"

"Yes, definitely." Remy's eyes danced. Ash looked back, as helpless as ever to resist. For a long moment, they smiled stupidly at each other over their breakfast, and Ash felt entirely content, not embarrassed at all.

**THEY** spent the rest of the day playing tourist. They went to Hatley, of course, to visit the castle, because "*X-Men* and *Smallville*, Ash," and Remy bought a key chain, grinning like a nutter the whole time.

They paid the entrance fee and wandered the gardens. When they found themselves out of view of the castle and of any other tourists, Remy reached out and tangled their fingers together. He laughed and smiled and, more ridiculously, lifted Ash's hand so he could kiss his fingers.

Foolishly, Ash let him. It didn't feel like anyone was watching here. It felt safe to be daft and affectionate, to let Remy hold his hand and snog him. Ash leaned in and pressed a quick kiss to the apple of Remy's cheek to watch the way he went pink and giggled.

At the pond, they crossed a bridge and found themselves so sheltered by trees and felt so alone that they couldn't help but come together for a long, passionate snog. Remy curled his fingers in Ash's hair, and Ash wrapped his hands around Remy's ribs.

"I've been longing to do that all day. Why didn't I when we were still at the hotel?"

"Because we never would have left"—Ash's heart thumped wildly against his ribs to say those words—"and you had to see the castle. Just had to," Ash murmured.

Remy chuckled, low and intimate. "Definitely wouldn't have left the room." He gave what Ash could only describe as bedroom eyes, lids low, and Ash shivered with pleasure and a sense of naughtiness—to be doing this in public, to do it at *all*. He gripped Remy tighter.

They wandered about the grounds so slowly it was well past noon by the time they returned to the main house and tried the café. After their plates were cleaned, Remy stubbornly insisted on paying the bill.

"Eating here was my idea," Ash pointed out reasonably.

"Yes, but you're covering everything this weekend. Let me at least pay for this?"

Ash didn't want to relent but conceded the argument when Remy handed his card over faster.

They headed back toward the hotel and wandered the harbor district in daylight, popping into shops and laughing like giddy children in store aisles. Over and over, Ash caught himself watching Remy. He wondered if Remy knew he glowed.

They had dinner in the hotel restaurant, tucked into a corner, candles on the table, their toes bumping together under cover of the cloth. Ash had never played footsie before.

And he definitely never had someone run the tops of their toes up and down his calf while they grinned at him over dishes of risotto and seafood.

"You've really never done this?"

Ash shook his head. "No. Never wanted to with anyone else."

"Aw, you sweet-talker, you." Remy winked, but it didnae disguise the rising heat in his gaze. "Now, please tell me we're not having dessert, because I would very much like to go back to our room so I can kiss you a lot."

So they did.

They snogged until their lips were bruised, Remy's cheeks pink from Ash's beard, and their shirts missing, until they were pressed tightly together, and Ash surprised them both by coming in his jeans, trembling and gasping and apologizing while Remy ran gentling hands over him.

Then, after Ash calmed down, Remy opened his trousers and undulated over him, rubbing his briefs-covered dick into Ash's hip until he too came, babbling Ash's name.

**THEY** stayed in bed Sunday morning. Ash ordered them more room service, then took the trays back to bed. They lounged together under the sheets, sipping coffee and tea and feeding each other fruit, cheese, and pastry between kisses.

Ash pulled up TripAdvisor on his phone, looking for something touristy to do, but Remy grabbed it and chucked it onto the nightstand.

"I'd rather stay right here," he murmured.

"But," Ash said, trying to pull away from Remy's lips and finding he had a severe lack of willpower, "don't you want to see more stuff while you're here?"

"I can come back," Remy said, somewhat savagely.

He pushed Ash onto his back and straddled his hips. Ash was rapidly learning how much he liked it—having Remy over him, his weight across his hips, letting Remy guide him through.

"But you're here *now*," he pointed out, not really protesting anymore. If Remy wanted to stay in bed until checkout, who was he to argue?

"Who cares?" Remy asked and kissed him before he could say more.

Several long, snog-filled moments later, they were forced apart in order to silence the obnoxious trilling of Ash's phone. He caught sight of the time and groaned.

"Checkout in half an hour."

Remy sighed regretfully, stood, and headed straight for the shower.

They rushed to get all their things into their bags, laughing as they threw items across the room to get them to their rightful owner.

"We have a few hours before we catch the bus to the ferry," Ash mentioned as they rode the lift down.

"Walk around the neighborhood?"

"Whatever you want."

Remy lunged forward to press a quick kiss to Ash's lips, but he pulled back in time for the doors to open. Ash shook his head and led the way to the lobby desk.

As they stood in the queue, Remy spotted his friends from the first day and said, "I'm gonna say goodbye," and left Ash alone. A fact for which he was grateful when he was presented with a bill well over two thousand dollars. Last-minute rooms were never cheap, he thought ruefully and vowed never to tell Remy.

That afternoon, as they settled on the bus for the ferry, he felt as though they were leaving a bubble, like they'd been living in a state unconnected to the real world. *Like an island?* he thought sarcastically and pushed away his maudlin thoughts.

Remy was warm and next to him, pressing their knees subtly together and asking Ash about the view out the window. The weekend had been amazing, yes, but that wouldn't stop or disappear when they got to Vancouver. They would still be dating, and life wisnae going to fall apart because they took a boat.

Ash pressed back, enjoying the weight, and focused on Remy's rambles about the clouds.

Vancouver could wait until they got there.

## Chapter Ten

**ETTA** drove Ash to work the following day.

Mondays were reserved for table reads of the latest script, last-minute reshoots, and for looping so the editors could touch up and add any missing audio from previous episodes.

They'd booked Ash for a recording stint right after the read, so Etta opted to work out at the studio.

"You got home late last night." She reached over to flick the script sitting in Ash's lap, which he had shamefully not finished reading.

"Yeah."

She waited for him to say more, but he wasn't sure where to start.

"You have a good weekend, then? Fun time on the island?"

"Yeah. Remy dragged me to see the castle at Hatley." He smiled fondly at the memory of Remy muttering about homoerotic symbolism and Lex Luthor.

"And of course you were happy to go see it again, you nerd."

"The grounds are beautiful," Ash defended. Yes, he'd gone to Hatley years before because of its role on film, but he never would let Remy drag him back if it weren't worth seeing. Or maybe he would if Remy wanted. Ash couldn't resist those eyes.

"Right," Etta drawled skeptically.

Ash narrowed his eyes. "How was *your* weekend?"

"Good." She drummed nervously on the steering wheel for a moment, then said, "Carlo at the gym asked me about teaching again."

"Oh?" Carlo had been after Etta to teach self-defense and aikido for ages, but Etta always said no, not ready for a job so much more social than the mostly quiet existence Ash offered.

"Yeah." *Rat-a-tat.* "I'm thinking I'll say yes. Just one class to start, but… it sounds nice."

*Good.* It would be good for her, and she was wasted hiding as his glorified companion. "You'll make a quality teacher."

"I hope so," she said, pulling into the car park. As she waited to be waved through the gate, she shot him a pleased smile, which he returned.

At the table read, Janet called them all to attention and announced, "Before we get started, I wanted to take a moment to congratulate you all on such a strong start. Only two episodes out, and we've already got a fan base and positive critical reviews."

A cheer went around the table.

"So give yourself a pat on the back for good work." She winked. Then her expression turned serious. "And I'm aware of the fuss some quarters are making, but those quarters are never happy, and they're forcing the fans to be vocal. So focus on the good, people, because I'm proud to be part of this project." She smiled and sat down, motioning for this week's director to take the reins.

After the read, Ash headed to audio, and throughout the somewhat dull process of rerecording lines, gasps, and grunts, he reminded himself about the love for the show.

"That's all for today," the tech said, releasing Ash midafternoon. And after a quick "Cheers, see you next week, Jialee," Ash hustled from the booth and pulled out his phone.

The text icon sat at the top of his screen. He clicked on Etta's conversation first but found nothing new there.

*All done. Meet at entrance?* he sent.

He found a text from Langston, pictures of the kids, both of them covered head-to-toe in mud. *Sure you don't miss Scottish rain?*

Ash typed back, *Snort, Vancouver isnae better. Cute pics though.*

Next came a text from Adele, ex-costar extraordinaire. She'd sent a shot of the California sunshine and *Strangely I still miss the rainy north. And you. Miss me?*

*Always. Come see me*, he wrote. The hardest part about *Restraint* ending had been the loss of his friends; several of his costars had left the city for other projects. He missed Adele the most, as she'd been such a constant in his life for those six years and they'd both been rubbish at staying in touch.

Last he found a text from Remy. *You're here today, right? Come see me in writer's room before you leave?*

Damn. Did he have time? Would Etta be annoyed if he asked for another twenty at least?

His phone pinged with a new message from Etta Haynes. *Give me thirty to shower.*

*Okay np,* he wrote to her, and *On my way* to Remy.

Tucked in a corner of the studio sat the writers' wing, a series of offices for writers' meetings and script doctors. Each office was a large room with a landline, several sockets, and a substantial conference table.

Ash found the door with a printed sign which said "Mythfits Writers' Room." Someone had written below in red Sharpie, *Enter at risk of faery curse*, and another smartass had added in black ink, *Beware of vampires, werewolves, and other beasties.*

The door was ajar, so Ash knocked and peered in. Remy was sat alone at the table, his brow furrowed and his laptop open and ignored as he wrote feverishly in a notebook.

"Hey?"

"Ash! You came!" His frown melted into a smile. "Give me a second to finish making notes about this? I don't want to forget."

Ash entered the room, nudged the door shut behind him, and waited until Remy stopped scribbling. "How goes it?"

"Okay, but so much better now you're here," Remy said impishly and hopped across the room. As Ash figured he would, Remy slung his arms around his shoulders and snogged him dirtily, openmouthed and with liberal tongue. "I've been thinking about that since I woke up. I had the dirtiest dream last night." He smiled wistfully.

"Yeah?" Ash prompted. He didn't know how to do this, but he was willing to be led.

"Hmm, yeah. We were tangled up in bed, I was riding you—" Ash's grip tightened involuntarily. "Like the idea, do you?"

Ash's mouth went dry. "I like everything with you."

"Sap," Remy said, but he kissed Ash again, so that couldn't be too terrible a thing.

They snogged until Ash's phone beeped in his pocket. Etta. "I have to go."

"Noooo," Remy whined.

"Etta is waiting."

"Let her wait longer. I need you more."

"You do?" Ash smiled, teasing, but his heart leapt at the thought of Remy needing him.

"Yeah. What's *she* doing? I'm researching monsters, trying to find candidates for episodes, and writing summaries on them and their powers and any suggestions for plots I might have."

"And that's—what? Boring?" Ash fought the smile tugging at his mouth.

"Yes."

"Liar. You love doing research."

Remy stuck out his bottom lip and widened his eyes, but Ash rolled his own and tucked that lip back in with a finger.

"More than a wee bit. So much so, I think maybe you're using it to avoid writing?"

Remy wrinkled his nose. "Maybe," he sulked.

"How goes it?"

"The writing? Shit as ever."

Ash pressed a kiss to Remy's forehead. "How about you come over after you're done here, and I'll feed you."

Remy narrowed his eyes. "Food that you're making?"

Ash snorted. "Well, I was going to make that chicken thing you showed me, but if you're going to be like that…."

"You're not ready to fly solo on the chicken thing."

"Ouch. Fine. What about sushi?"

"Ooh, I love sushi." Remy wiggled happily, leaned into him further, and pressed a quick kiss to his lips. "Salmon maki? And tuna rolls? Oh, and extra wasabi and ginger."

"Salmon, tuna, wasabi, ginger. Got it."

"You're the best boyfriend ever," Remy sighed.

Ash's stomach jumped and his heart pounded. *Boyfriend.* "Aye," he rasped and cleared his throat. "And dinnae forget it."

"Never," Remy said in that dreamy tone. Then he pressed one last kiss to Ash's lips before stepping away and pushing him towards the door. "Now go and buy me lots of sushi. I'll see you around six?"

"Six," Ash promised and left. Then he made his way to the front door and Etta. He should probably be more circumspect, but try as he might, he couldn't get the smile off his face.

**ASH** put the leftover salad in the fridge, loaded the plates into the dishwasher, and turned to the living room. He paused at the breakfast bar and stared at Remy curled on the couch. He'd settled with his back on the armrest, his chin resting on his knees, and was reading a book propped on a pillow at his feet. Ash smiled as Remy flipped a page, scoffed, read for a moment, muttered at the book, then turned another page. Not wanting to disturb him, Ash stayed put.

He couldn't believe it had already been a week since their rendezvous in Victoria—a week of stolen kisses in Ash's dressing room and Remy's office, of dinners at Ash's place, of meals in the cafeteria where they kept their distance but sneaked heated looks, of tea breaks in secluded corners, of learning Remy's body and what Remy liked, of discovering what he liked himself, and most surprising of all, with some nights spent tangled up in the same sheets, partially clothed but still reveling in the intimacy. Ash couldn't believe how lovely it was to simply sleep with someone, to spend the last moments of the day knowing they'd be the first person you'd see upon waking. He loved it, even when he woke up in the middle of the night bruised and wondering if he wasn't risking his life being in such close quarters with an unconscious Remy. But he knew he'd never want to give it up. Better to be bruised and with Remy than unscathed without him.

On the couch, Remy huffed and wrinkled his nose. Ash smiled. Not even the increasingly irate idiots on the internet could get him to stop smiling this week.

A few minutes later, Remy frowned, reached down into his messenger bag, and pulled out a small laptop. He snapped it open, perused the screen, and started tapping furiously.

Wanting to soothe those lines, Ash made his way over to the couch. He settled at Remy's feet and waited until he had finished typing. "Y'alright?"

Remy lifted his gaze, focused on Ash, and smiled without humor. "Fine. Just… frustrated."

"Your script?"

"Two steps forwards, two back, you know?" He sighed gustily. "Maybe I should chuck it."

Ash smoothed the frown lines out of Remy's forehead. "No. Don't. I'm sure it's good." He'd offered to read it several times, but Remy always refused, so Ash kept mum on that topic now. "That werewolf puppy episode was fantastic."

"I didn't write it," Remy pointed out.

"Maybe not the full thing, but the story was your idea. Don't worry about the dialogue being perfect—focus on the story and it'll be fine." He placed his hand on Remy's foot and gently stroked his ankle.

Remy tilted his head and regarded him. "Sweet-talker." He sighed. "But it doesn't change the fact that I can't get the plot to work."

"Tell me about it?" Ash asked gently, trying to keep any presumption from his tone.

Remy chewed his lip and then, to Ash's surprise, did just that. "It's about the lightning bird. They're African, shape-shifters, and often a witch's familiar." He licked his abused lip. "I'm not sure where to go with it."

"Hmm." Ash twisted and settled so he sat facing Remy, but kept his hand settled on Remy's foot. "Tell me more about the lightning bird?"

"Oh. Um, let's see. Well, it's a bird, obviously, unless it's taken human shape. It can summon thunder and lightning. Sometimes it's a vampire, with an unending thirst for blood, and sometimes a witch's familiar. Oh, and sometimes they're immortal, so they get passed down through the witch family."

"Mm. Kind of like Hamish?"

Remy jerked, stared at Ash for a moment, blinked, then smiled. "Yes. Exactly like Hamish. I think this plot just got so much better. Obviously this lightning bird character should parallel Hamish's story. He's supposed to mostly interact with Niall and Roxanne—vampire bird and all—but well, Hamish details always work in a Niall story." Remy winked.

For some reason Ash didn't understand, he blushed. Ridiculous. It wasn't as if he *were* Hamish or had any real control over Hamish's brewing romance with Niall. Yet the wink made him embarrassed and guilty.

"Are you blushing?"

"Stuff it."

"No, no! Why are you blushing?" Remy's smile dimmed. "Seriously, why the red cheeks?" He reached out and swept a thumb over one.

"Only…." Ash swallowed. "It doesn't bother you?"

"What?" Remy frowned.

Ash gestured vaguely. "The… *romance*."

"The Hamish and Niall story? No? I think it's awesome the show's so queer."

Ash frowned. He'd known Remy approved of the story line, but surely he'd changed his mind now they were dating. "Yes. But they'll snog eventually. Maybe not this series, but Janet doesn't want to wait too long, says she doesn't want to *X-Files* it."

Remy snorted. "That's good. And it doesn't bother me. I mean, okay, it's not going to be *great* seeing you kiss another guy now, but I know it's not you. It's Hamish. And to be honest"—he shrugged—"I ship it. Hamish and Niall are adorable."

Ash rolled his eyes and grumbled.

"No, they really are. The cutest," Remy insisted. "Mostly because Niall is smitten and Hamish has no idea. Also Hamish is kind of innocent for something that's a few hundred years old. Very adorable blushes."

"I'm no' 'adorable,'" Ash said, affronted.

"Of course you are! And I've got legions of Zvi fans who agree with me. The most adorable."

"They do not," Ash protested. He tended to avoid googling himself, because he had a fair idea of what kinds of words were being used to describe him—*sexy* being one of the tamer ones—and didn't want to see anything in graphic black and white. But he was fairly certain no one had ever attached *adorable* to his name, not when he'd been playing a werewolf with such a turbulent past as to leave him brooding and prone to violent outbursts, among other less-than-appealing attributes.

Remy laughed. He moved the book and notebook off the sofa, shifted his body, and then knee-walked the few feet across the pillows to settle astride Ash's lap. His long legs around Ash's hips sent his thoughts spiraling. "Don't be so grumpy. It's a good thing, I promise. You are the most adorable." He pressed several fleeting kisses to Ash's mouth and face. "You have an adorable mouth." He kissed it again. "Cute pout too." Kiss. "And blushes on your ridiculous cheekbones." Kiss, kiss. "Or along your rugged, manly bearded jaw." Kiss, kiss, kiss.

Ash gasped at the lingering lips on the edge of his jaw, below his ear—who knew that would feel so lovely?—and wrapped one hand around Remy's head and the other around his ribs and held him close.

He turned and brought their mouths together, and for several delicious moments, neither of them said anything.

"Still think I'm *adorable*?" Ash panted into the moist air between their mouths.

"Excessively. You're still hot like burning and sexy as hell too, though," Remy said. He shimmied his hips, bumping their groins together and ending the debate for the night. Which was fine. Ash could always try dissuading Remy another day.

## *Chapter Eleven*

**ASH** yawned and handed Etta another dish for the washer. Despite the restful and wonderful weekend with Remy—who still refused to concede on the adorable front—three days at work and he was tired again, probably because they'd had two dawn shootings, which meant fairly early call times in mid-June.

A knock sounded on the front door, startling Ash with a rapid tattoo that kept up, unchecked, until Ash, his eyes wide, opened it.

Remy stood on the other side, beaming. "Hey." He bounced on his toes. "Guess what."

"What?" Ash smiled, stepped back, and let him into the flat.

Remy bounded in. "Hi, Etta. Guess what!"

Etta dried her hands. "You've started taking speed?"

"Nope." Remy pressed his lips together and continued to bounce.

His joy was infectious. "You gonna tell us?"

Remy bounced on the balls of his feet and clapped his hands together, and the words spilled out. "They liked my script. I finished it and gave it to them, and they liked it." He did a little dance, feet shuffling and fists waving. "Janet says she wants to keep it for season two, if we get one. She wants to put my script on TV."

"Congrats," Etta said, smiling.

Ash nodded. "Terrific." Unable to stop himself, he surged forward, wrapped a hand around Remy's neck, and pulled him in for a kiss. He licked in just the way Remy liked, a dirty tease and promise. *Later.* "That's amazing," he whispered.

Remy vibrated. "Isn't it?"

"Yeah." Ash kissed him again and swept his thumb across Remy's cheekbone. "Fantastic news."

"Thanks." Remy leaned up, his turn for a kiss. "Thanks to you. Never would have finished it without your help," he murmured.

Ash shook his head. "Not true."

"Okay, I never would have finished it so *quickly*," Remy countered and kissed him again—probably to stop any more arguments. "I definitely *owe* you. Hmm, maybe you'll let me suck you?" His lips brushed Ash's burning ears.

"Oh." They hadn't done that yet, but Ash *wanted*.

"Tonight." Remy pulled back, tangled their fingers together, and swung their hands. "Wanna bake some cookies to celebrate?"

"Yes," Etta said. Ash jumped.

"Er, what sort of cookie?" he recovered.

"Hmm, I was thinking peanut butter–chocolate chip if you have the ingredients."

Etta snorted. "If you haven't figured it out by now, Ash's kitchen always has peanut butter and chocolate."

Ash scowled and hoped he wasn't actually blushing. Curse his ginger skin. "They're sweeties I'm allowed." Or rather, ones he could work into his diet. A square of dark chocolate was one of his favorite treats.

Remy shook his head. "Oh, honey. Peanut butter is not a sweet."

Ash turned his frown onto Remy. "It's full of fat. And sugars."

"There, there." Remy patted his arm. "Don't worry. I'm going to make you the best peanut-butter cookies you ever had." He strode into the kitchen. "Do you know where he hides the chocolate?"

Smiling, Etta reached up to a cupboard's top shelf for an extra-large bag of chocolate chips from Costco.

Remy grinned. "Perfect." He clapped his hands together. "Ash, get over here and help. Cooking-lesson time."

"This isn't cooking," Ash grumbled but complied.

"I don't care," Remy singsonged. "Baking, cooking. We're making cookies and celebrating my awesomeness."

"Well, if you put it like that," Ash said. He pressed a kiss to Remy's forehead and then fetched the peanut butter out of the fridge.


ASH placed the candles, lit them, and looked over the table. Plates, cutlery, glasses, napkins, wine... everything was ready. He went to the kitchen to peek into the oven and check on dinner.

"I'm off," Etta said as she marched from her bedroom to the doorway. "I won't be back until late tonight. But I am coming back—midnight—so keep that in mind." Her voice was stern, but she smirked and waved on her way out the door, ignoring his spluttering indignation.

As the door clicked shut behind her, he let out a sigh of relief. He felt bad about kicking her out, but she *had* volunteered. And she was off to a girls' night with some new colleagues, not to hide lonely in some gym or twenty-four-hour diner. Still…. He'd make her favorite as a thank-you—waffles from scratch, like Remy had taught him.

He glanced at the timer again and then rubbed his hands over his face. The silence of the flat felt… dangerous. Too much time to think.

He turned from the table, looking for a distraction, but his brain took the opportunity to linger on life's other stressors.

Work had been weird all week—ever since Tuesday, the day after Remy's announcement, when Ash ran into Janet in the hallway. She'd been whispering heatedly into her phone before she spotted Ash, gave him a perfunctory, polite smile, and rushed away. Worried for her, Ash forced himself to push the incident from his mind, not wanting to pry, but then came the script incident.

Production aimed to give them scripts as soon as possible, usually Friday afternoon, but late in the day, production informed them the latest wasn't finished. When Michael asked why, Janet admitted, somewhat tight-faced, that the higher-ups had rejected next week's story. Not to worry, though, they would all receive their scripts via courier that weekend.

The one time a *Restraint* suit had nixed an episode hadn't exactly been good news.

Ash huffed. *Worry nae'er solved anay man's woes*, as Maw'd always said.

Thankfully a knock on the door kept him from wandering farther down *that* unhappy lane. Ash jumped and hurried to answer it.

"Hey," Remy said. He stepped in, leaned up for a lingering kiss, and handed him a plastic container with something chocolatey-looking inside.

"Hello. What's this?"

"Chocolate shortbread covered in chocolate."

Ash narrowed his eyes at Remy's innocent face. "Ye ken I dinnae huv tae like shortbread jist 'cause I'm Scottish, aye?"

"Of course not, dear." He patted Ash's arm and moved into the kitchen. Then, apparently noticing the table, he stopped and stared. After a long pause, during which Ash did a lot of sweating, he asked, "Is there a special occasion I forgot about?"

Ash swallowed. "Well, you wrote your first script…." Ash *had* consulted Etta about the evening's plans and asked her which of the dishes he should make. But perhaps making a fuss wasn't the right thing? "I thought we could—hmph."

Remy launched himself at Ash, lips-first. Ash wound his left arm around him and opened his mouth, gladly accepting the dirty snog. He wished his right hand weren't already full, because, with Remy's tongue stroking his own, he wanted to do nothing else but pick him up and press their bodies even closer.

*Beep beep beep.*

Ash jumped and remembered himself. "Dinner," he whispered. "I have to—it'll burn."

"Burning. Bad," Remy said huskily. Then he shook himself and stepped away, but his hands lingered on Ash's chest. "I should let you…. Dinner, right?"

"Right." Ash took a deep breath and might have gone back in for another kiss—Remy's gaze smoldered—but the incessant beeping could not be ignored. He stepped back and whispered, "Later. Dinner first."

Dinner was surprisingly passable, if Ash did say so himself. He'd learned so much from Remy in the kitchen, and he had fun showing off his new skills.

Remy swallowed a bite and loaded more on his fork. "This is good. Excellent chicken and roasted veggies."

"Thanks. No' as good as yours yet, but getting there."

Remy smirked. "No one's roasted veggies are as good as mine."

Ash rolled his eyes. "Yes, darling."

Remy sighed dreamily. "Your reluctance to believe anything I say is so charming. Definitely the reason I'm falling for you."

Ash stilled. He went hot, then cold, then hot again. His heart beat triple time and thought about escaping his chest. He licked his lips. *Falling for you.* Remy was falling for him—falling in *love.* He cleared his throat. "And here I though' ye were intae my werewolf past."

"Well, that was the reason I started talking to you," Remy conceded, "but it was your complete irreverence for me that kept me coming back, pumpkin."

Ash shook his head and looked down at his dinner. "Well, in that case, I guess I better be doing it more often. Wouldn't want you to get bored or decide to leave." He looked up from under his lashes to see how Remy took his statement.

He pinked but grinned. "Good idea."

For a moment Ash could hardly breathe for the happiness bubbling and exploding inside him. "I thought so," he murmured, then leaned over to swipe a kiss across those pouty lips.

"I'm done eating," Remy whispered.

"Oh?" Ash pressed a kiss to the corner of his mouth, his cheek.

"Absolutely." Remy pushed his plate away and kissed Ash's nose. "Dinner is done. And who's ready for dessert? Not me. Definitely not... me...." He landed a few more brushes of lips to Ash's face between words.

"Yeah." Ash ran his fingers through Remy's hair, and Remy sighed in contentment and rubbed his head against Ash's hand.

"Right, so... bedroom?" Remy's eyes fluttered open, and he stared at Ash uncertainly. How could he think Ash would say no?

Ash nodded without hesitation. "Bedroom."

They stumbled together from the dining room, clumsy with their efforts to keep touching. It wasn't like the passionate stumble of film, but a slow, stuttering shuffle. Every few steps, they stalled out, too focused on touching to think about walking. Sometimes they stopped to remove some clothes, but mostly they got distracted by their need to touch, caressing for the joy of it.

It was far from Remy's first visit to Ash's bedroom, and yet... something about it felt brand-new, different.

Over the past two weeks, they'd stumbled their way through teen stuff—the sort of things most people did in dorm rooms—but they'd mostly kept their clothes on, even last Wednesday, after they baked cookies, when Remy sidled down the bed and promised he wasn't expecting Ash to reciprocate, but could he please suck his cock? Or after, when Ash wrapped his hand around Remy's bare flesh and stroked until Remy came all over Ash's T-shirt.

But somehow Ash knew that tonight everything would come off, all barriers would be removed.

He skimmed his hands up Remy's body and dragged his shirt up, off, and away. Remy was warm and soft under his hands, his skin smooth but for the sparse hair across his chest.

Remy made quick work of the buttons on Ash's shirt, then followed his hands with his lips and lay kisses along the way. Ash watched his slow progress downward and gasped, overcome by the sight of Remy's lips on his skin, the contrast of their coloring—Remy already summer tanned in this wet June, and Ash winter pale. His knees trembled. He placed his hands on Remy's head—to touch, to ground himself, not to push or guide. Remy looked up at him, smirked, and pressed a kiss to Ash's belly. Then he stood and pushed the shirt off Ash's shoulders.

Ash didn't watch it flutter to the floor, too busy staring at Remy's big beautiful eyes and wondering what he planned next.

They wiggled out of their jeans, and Remy giggled as Ash untangled his from his feet—skinny jeans made his ass and thighs look amazing, but they weren't easy to take off—and then they settled on the bed, still in their underwear.

They curled on their sides, facing each other, bare legs brushing. It wasn't a new sensation, but this time felt different. They'd cuddled up before, but always for sleeping or frotting, never as a prelude to *more*.

They snogged until Ash's mouth bruised and Remy was pink from Ash's beard.

"What," Remy gasped, "do you want to do?"

"Everything."

Remy chuckled, low and throaty. "What about—can I ride you?"

Ash groaned and tightened his grip on Remy's hips. "Ye—d'ye want tae?"

"Yes," Remy breathed. "I've been thinking about it, dreaming about it." He ran a hand through Ash's hair and smirked. "Fantasized about it for years, to be honest. I used to imagine it, back before I met you, when jerking off with my favorite toy." Ash made a choked noise and pulled Remy closer. Their hips collided deliciously. "Felt guilty about it after last year... less so after meeting you again." He grinned, arched his back, and rubbed their groins together. "Definitely no bad feelings about it in the past few weeks. Ever since—I've been dreaming about it."

A very unmanly noise burst out of Ash's throat, and he lunged forward for a sloppy kiss. He couldn't imagine Remy with a-a sex toy... or well, he could, all too vividly.

"So, do you want to?" Remy gasped.

"Aye."

Remy gave that low husky laugh again, and heat curled in Ash's belly.

It felt... easy then. Not that everything went smoothly—Ash dropped the lube and nearly fell out of bed trying to grab it, and Remy almost kneed him in the balls at one point, which resulted in more giggles—but the blunders didn't make him self-conscious. In a funny way, they made everything feel more real.

Remy led and Ash followed. He straddled Ash's hips and covered his fingers in lube and worked them in, stretching himself.

Ash rested his hands on Remy's thighs and watched him, transfixed. He'd thought about it, sure, but he hadn't known….

"Fuuuck," Remy sighed, apparently pleased with the angle. "I'm, I'm ready. Get—where's the condom?"

Right, condom. Ash found the packet in the drawer—the first in a new box, purchased the other day in anticipation, the first he'd ever bought.

He fumbled with the foil, struggled to open it, and then hesitated. Those lessons as a teen when he'd rolled one onto a banana had been a long time ago.

Remy huffed a laugh. "The look on your face." He leaned forward and kissed Ash on the mouth. "So confused. I've never seen a man look so lost by a glove before." He slipped it from Ash's fingers and reached down to roll it on. Ash grunted and gritted his teeth, for a moment sure he'd come from the sensation of Remy brushing the latex down his length, but it was nothing compared to how it felt when Remy raised himself to his knees, positioned Ash, and slowly sank onto him. Nor could anything compare to the sight of Remy with his head tossed back, his mouth open, his eyes shut, as he gasped, sighed, and moaned all the way down.

Ash panted and stared. His mind blanked. His grip on Remy's hips went lax. The feeling of tight and hot around him and the vision of Remy above him were all he could take in, all he could process. He gaped.

When Remy was all the way down, he settled on Ash's hips, petted his chest, and breathed deep. "Hey," he sighed, smiling.

Ash swallowed and rasped, "'Lo."

Remy chuckled—and that felt weird… but good. Then he bent down for a kiss, which Ash returned eagerly. He leaned up into it and pressed his tongue forward.

When Remy pulled back to sit up, Ash tried to follow, lifting his head and shoulders off the bed before he realized.

Grinning and panting, Remy sat back, winked at Ash, then lifted his hips.

Ash swore.

Then, when Remy was almost all the way off, he got even tighter and slowly pressed all the way back down. Ash went cross-eyed.

"Jee-sus," he breathed.

"Nope. Just me," Remy said with a smirk, like it wasn't the lamest joke ever. And Ash loved him.

Heart thumping, Ash rolled his eyes and tightened his fingers around Remy's hips, but it was a suggestion, not a command. He didn't push.

Remy smiled at him, all confidence, then rose once more. Ash held on. Soon Remy worked himself in a steady rhythm, alternating the angle of his hips until he found one which forced the most amazing moans out of his slack mouth.

For a moment Ash almost forgot the tight friction pushing him to orgasm as he stared transfixed at Remy's beautiful face. He couldn't believe….

He pulled his body up, head and torso, to bring his face within range. "Kiss me?"

Remy obliged. He stilled his hips and leaned forward until their mouths met. The kiss was awkward—openmouthed, panting, uncoordinated—and yet not. Neither of them was very smooth right then.

Remy wrapped his arms around Ash's shoulders, and Ash pushed himself up into a seated position.

They resettled, kissing the whole while, gasping and laughing when they stumbled. They were wrapped up together, Ash still inside Remy and Remy's limbs around him, holding him close. Then Remy started to… undulate, not really fucking himself so much as grinding their hips together, creating friction with the barest of movement, and bumping his dick up against Ash's belly.

It was amazing. Tangled up together, in each other, sharing this moment only they were part of. No one else could know them or this moment the way they did.

Ash came, trembling, held firmly in Remy's arms, his face buried in Remy's neck. And after, he wrapped one arm around Remy's waist to hold him tight and reached down to stroke him the way he was learning Remy liked, until Remy too gasped and came, shuddering and shaking.

After they unwound their embrace and tidied up a bit, they lay together in a tangle of sheets, cuddling close, and Ash thought nothing could ever be better.


**THEY** woke up before midnight. Ash pressed a kiss to Remy's lips and murmured, "Stay right here." He put on his robe and went in search of dessert.

He was pulling glasses out of the cupboard when he heard the front door unlock. Etta walked in, and he was caught in the act. Wearing nothing but a robe, holding two glasses, and with a tray next to him already laden with shortbread and milk, Ash became acutely aware of how he must look to her: thoroughly shagged.

His face heated. Unable to move his arms to put down the glasses, he was stuck in an odd pantomime when she caught sight of him.

"Hey," she said quietly. "How was the date?" She glanced at the tray and smiled.

Ash blinked. He should run. Though… a small, surprising part of him wanted to tell her everything—not in detail or to brag, but just to share. "It was *really* good," he blurted. And then wanted to sink into the floor.

Etta grinned wide. "Good. I'm glad you had a 'really good' *date*."

Ash swallowed, mouth dry. "Thanks. Erm, how was your night?"

"Great. The ladies are awesome." She kicked off her shoes and hung up her coat. "We went to Chellie's for pizza and beer, watched *Jupiter Ascending* and *Wonder Woman*." She covered up a yawn. "Anyway. It's bedtime. Enjoy the rest of your date." She winked and waved at him as she sauntered through the flat toward her door. "Night, Remy," she called softly as she passed by the door to the master suite.

"Night" came the choked-laughter response.

Face burning, Ash finally got unstuck, placed the glasses on the tray, and hurried back to his room, where Remy was lounging on the bed. He sat propped up on pillows, with only his groin and one leg covered by the sheet, in a manner which might grace the front of a romance novel, and he was shaking with silent laughter.

Ash shut the door firmly behind him—using his behind—and rested against it for a moment. He glared halfheartedly. "Stuff it, you," he grumbled, which only made Remy laugh harder.

"Oh God. It was funny before, but now that I see your face…." He gave an exaggerated wipe to one cheek, as if brushing away tears. "So good."

Ash narrowed his eyes. Then he strode across the room, put the tray on his bedside table, and crawled onto the mattress. He straddled Remy's thighs and looked down at him. "What about my face?" he asked, putting in a bit of Zvi's growl.

Remy shivered, and his eyes went wide. Then he cupped Ash's face in warm palms, murmured, "Nothing. It's lovely," and leaned in for a long, slow kiss.

"As much as I'd love to explore this further," Remy murmured as their noses bumped together, "you brought me dessert." He leaned back and away, stretched his torso across the pillows, and reached for the cookies.

Surprised, Ash didn't react until Remy already had a bite in his mouth. "Gee, thanks," he drawled.

"No prob." Remy stuffed his half-eaten cookie into Ash's mouth. Reflexively Ash bit, chewed, and moaned. The shortbread was flaky and sweet with a taste of cocoa. The chocolate layer on top was dark and rich, and was that a hint of salt?

Remy nodded. "Yeah. I sprinkled some sea salt on top." He looked thoughtful. "I like it."

"Oh, well, if *you* like it...."

"Look, we all know I'm the food guy in this relationship."

Ash's mind went to mush. "Aye. Ye are." And he leaned in for a chocolate-sweet kiss.

## Chapter Twelve

**THEY** woke late the next morning. Ash found himself camped on the edge of the mattress, as usual, and he smiled softly. Then he got out of bed, cleaned up in his en suite to make himself presentable enough for Etta, threw on joggers and a tee, and headed out to make breakfast. Remy would want to make them omelets, but by now Ash knew well enough how to prepare veggies for them.

When Remy emerged, hair tousled and eyelids heavy, he was wrapped in Ash's robe. Ash swallowed. For all the nights Remy had stayed over, he'd never borrowed clothes before.

"Morning."

"Morning," Remy murmured, his voice sleep rough. He pressed up to place a tender kiss to the corner of Ash's mouth and then rumbled a sleep-zombie–like, "Coffeeee," and moved on.

Remy made omelets, and they sat at the breakfast bar to eat them. Per their new habits, Ash grabbed his latest book and flipped it open, and Remy read the news on his phone.

Ash had pushed his plate aside and pulled *Hidden Figures* closer, and was lingering with his second cup of tea when Remy grunted a noise of surprise. Ash looked over and saw Remy frowning at his phone as he typed quickly. After his thumbs stilled, Ash hummed an inquiry.

"Nothing. Just… an email from an old prof. Was surprised to hear from him."

Ash waited for more, but Remy shook his head and changed the subject.

"I heard from Nisha. She's being sent to a conference in Winnipeg." He wrinkled his nose. "Apparently it was in Vancouver last year." He sighed gustily. "Just my luck."

Ash pressed a consoling kiss to his forehead. "Maybe she can come for a holiday? Maybe later this summer or in the fall."

"Maybe," Remy said slowly, though he didn't sound confident.

Ash cleared his throat. "I've got the office… I know it's a small room, but it's big enough to crash in if she wants."

The somewhat subdued mood fell away, and Remy smiled at him with such tenderness that Ash struggled not to look away. "Ashland Wells, you are a treasure and a sweet man. I've no idea what I've done to deserve you."

Ash colored. "Don't be daft. She's your dearest friend. How could I not put her up?"

Remy smiled. "Indeed." Then he leaned in and pressed several happy kisses to Ash's willing mouth.

**OVER** the course of the next week, Ash tried to hold on to those memories of being warm and cozy in his kitchen, as he spent several nights stuck in a public park thanks to the latest episode. Darn vampires and their need for night shoots. Though he supposed he should be grateful *Mythfits* didn't have nearly as many calls on location or during the night as *Restraint*. They'd had a bit of a dark and gloomy obsession, and during those six years, Ash had miraculously grown even paler—to makeup's discontent—while hidden away from the sun.

On the second night in the park, Janet showed up and watched them for an hour. She stood on the sidelines, her expression pinched and unhappy, and stayed silent even after the director called cut.

By the following night, Ash was shattered and looking a little racoon-eyed. He was ready for a long night's sleep and the weekend.

*We're still on tomorrow right?* Remy texted on Friday, and Ash answered with a *Yes* before falling into bed.

Ash woke up late on Saturday and cursed when he saw the clock read half eleven. He rushed through the day's to-do list, without Etta's help as she was teaching, and barely got home from the grocery store before Remy arrived.

They settled in the kitchen, where Ash chopped vegetables and meat and shredded cheese under Remy's directions while Remy made up some sauce and mixed up pizza dough.

He was pulling it out of the bowl to knead by hand when his phone chimed on the counter. Remy cleaned off his hands and then frowned as he read the text.

"Hey, Nish and I were supposed to hang out tomorrow, but she has to cancel—family stuff. Do you mind if we chat a bit now?" He chewed his lip.

Ash tried not to frown at the veg—he didn't want Remy to misinterpret the reason—and said, "Of course I don't mind. I told you she's welcome here."

"Thank you," he murmured and kissed Ash's cheek. He propped up his phone, dialed, and Nisha's face appeared.

"Hey. How are you?"

Ash zoned out of the conversation and got lost in the rhythm of chopping—while his technique had improved, he was still laughably slow—and let Remy and Nisha have their time together.

When Ash ran out of things to chop, he tuned back in to discover Remy pressing the dough into pans as he chatted about the Hollmans' French bulldogs.

Ash settled next to him at the counter, waiting for further direction.

"Thanks for buying the groceries," Remy said and kissed his cheek. Ash glanced at the tablet. Nisha wore a smile. Happiness curled in his belly at being seen like this.

Feeling daring, he set his hand on Remy's hip, out of view of the camera, and squeezed. "No worries."

Remy smiled and leaned into him, and Ash settled his arm comfortably around Remy's waist. He took a sip of his wine.

"Don't you look happy," Nisha said over her own wineglass.

Remy hummed in agreement. "How's work? Anything new and exciting?"

She nodded and told them about working on the launch material for a game she couldn't yet name or describe in public.

Ash tilted his head to rest his cheek against Remy's curls. They'd grown long, unshorn since Remy's move.

"What about you? Still enjoying a life of unsecure employment?" Nisha asked.

Remy frowned at her. "Yes," he gritted. "It's a good job, lots of good people." He leaned into Ash.

"Right." Nisha gave a knowing look. "With no guarantee of advancement or stability—just what you were hoping for."

Remy wrinkled his nose. "Don't remind me."

Ash squeezed him. "Janet wants to use your script next year. Might lead to more."

"She said she wants the rights so she can *maybe* use it next year *if* there is another season," Remy pointed out.

"Still," Ash said.

"That's awesome. Why didn't I know about this?" Nisha demanded.

Remy's cheeks pinked. "It just happened. And there's a good chance it won't lead to anything. I mean, *Mythfits* has to get picked up for season two, and even if it does, the showrunners have to still want to do it and it has to fit with the plan, and—"

"It's still a victory," Ash said softly.

"Definitely," Nisha agreed.

Remy shrugged and smiled. "I guess."

"You start your novel yet?"

"Novel?" The only time Remy had ever mentioned writing a book had been in jest.

Remy waved him off. "She's not serious."

"Yes, I am." Nisha pointed at him. "I'm always serious when it comes to following your dreams."

Remy rolled his eyes. "It's not like that."

"Right, you've only been saying 'when I write a book' for ages, but you don't actually want to do it." She sighed and turned to Ash. "See what he's like? I know he wants to."

"Do you?"

"Maybe," Remy said, but it sounded like yes. "But who makes a living at that? Besides, don't let Nisha fool you. She just wants to say she knows an author." He stuck out his tongue.

She grinned. "It's true. I really want to brag about it. I've already been telling people my friend writes for TV."

"Of course you are." Remy shook his head.

Ash excused himself to the bathroom. Finished, he opened the door, then paused. Remy and Nisha were whispering heatedly enough to be heard across the open plan.

"—want to be sure you're sure about him."

"Yes. I am," Remy said firmly.

There was nowhere to hide in the flat, and feeling awkward, Ash slowly stepped out of the bathroom. Remy spotted him, smiled, and said a little louder, "I should let you go. Almost pizza time."

"Uh-huh. Good to meet you again, Ash," Nisha said. Then after lots of "love yous," Remy hung up.

"Thanks for that," he said. Ash waved it away. "No, talking to her means a lot to me, and I would have been bummed to miss her this weekend. So thank you."

"I wouldn't say no," Ash pointed out.

"I know but…. Look, it's not like I know a lot of people around here, so these calls are important."

Ash stepped in close and pressed a hand to Remy's cheek. "I get it." He kissed Remy's forehead. "Are you… are you lonely here?"

Remy shrugged. "Not when I'm with you."

"I'm glad." He kissed his lips. "But that didnae answer my question."

"A little. I mean, most of the other writers work from home, and I tried to find a beer league, but it's the wrong season. Meeting people to make friends when you don't have school is hard," he added, sounding bewildered.

"Well, you have me," Ash said, and Remy nodded. "And Etta. And the cast. They all love you. And that has nothing to do with me. Actually I think they might like you better."

Remy laughed. "They do not."

"Hmm. I'm pretty sure they do—and I cannae blame them. You're very likeable."

"Am I?"

"Yup. I've no doubt that after you've been here for longer than a couple of months, you'll be well-popular. I'll have to schedule you in advance."

"Never," Remy swore dramatically. "I'll always have time for you."

They were mid-snog and Ash was wondering how to ask for more when the timer sounded.

"That's the pizza," Remy murmured.

"One last kiss." Ash brushed their lips softly together.

"Pizza," Remy laughed and pulled away.

Right, time for dinner. And it would be a shame if their hard work burned. Better to put the snogging on hold.

There was always later.

**BY** the time Ash arrived at work on Monday morning for the table read, he was rested and ready for another week. Days off with Remy cured all.

The regular cast and crew, but none of the guest stars, were gathered around the table when Janet arrived.

She wore an expression even more pinched and unhappy as she settled into a chair, every one of her fortysomething years writ large.

"What's going on?" Michael asked.

Janet sighed. "Bad news. The network has decided that we're too hot to handle, too 'controversial.'" She blew out a breath, and Ash's stomach sank. "As of today, they're quietly pulling us off the air."

## *Chapter Thirteen*

**ASH** ate another spoonful of ice cream and watched Jonathan kick the jerkface off *Cake Wars*. Ash had waited all series for the talentless idiot to get his just desserts, but he took little satisfaction from it.

He ate more vanilla ice cream and frowned at the carton. He loved vanilla, but it wasn't best for moping.

A knock sounded at the door.

"It's open."

Remy walked in, his shoulders slumped. "Hey."

"Hey."

Remy kicked off his trainers, shuffled across the flat, and flopped onto the couch. "Today sucks."

"Aye."

"Why—" He cleared his throat. "I knew TV was fickle, but…."

"Yeah." Ash handed over the tub and spoon. "Yer subject to other people's whims in this business. One person green-lights ye, and another bins ye."

"'Bins'?" Remy blinked. "Have you been drinking?"

"Two beers. Etta said was too pathetic to drink more 'an that 'fore four." Ash slumped and leaned toward Remy.

"Right."

"Too shattered to 'member Canadian."

Remy gave a weak smile. "If I wasn't so sad and worried right now, that adorable sentence would have gotten you laid."

Ash swallowed, and though he was no' in the mood either, he enjoyed for a moment the thought of bare skin pressed together, Remy slick and—

"Where's Etta?"

"Getting tea. And more ice cream."

"Oh. That's nice of her."

"Aye." Ash nodded. "Though she says it's to save her from negligence charges, else I'd waste away."

Remy snorted, shimmied closer, put his head on Ash's shoulder, and passed him the spoon. "What are we watching?"

Ash looked at the TV and squinted. The program had changed. "I'm no' sure."

Remy snorted again. On-screen a woman plated fish and covered it with… chocolate drizzle?

"What?"

"Ah dunno. Change the channel?"

Ash grunted and Remy swiped the remote from the coffee table. "We need comfort viewing," he announced.

Twenty minutes later Etta found them cuddled together and watching the season two premiere of *Supergirl*.

She shook her head at them but didn't hesitate to join or share the sushi.

**"THE** fans are pissed," Remy said the following morning at breakfast.

News of the cancellation had leaked the night before.

Etta snorted into her ginger-lemon tea. "Of course they are."

"You should see some of these comments."

Ash shrugged and kept his head down. Not today. He wasn't ready. He stared hard at his open book, trying to focus on the words. He'd pulled out *Awake and Dreaming* because he didn't have the energy for anything but children's lit.

Maybe he couldn't manage even that.

"Shit. This thread has twenty tweets."

"About?" Etta cocked her head.

"Mostly about the homogeny of Hollywood. Damn. This is some well-worded and intelligent ire." Remy ran his finger up the tablet. "'Once again a show underrepresenting straight white dudes gets pulled for upsetting the very same.'"

Etta held up a fist for Remy to bump. "Nice."

Ash bit his lip and scowled at his blurring pages. He blinked several times and tried not to think about all the others—the people who hated them, *him*, enough to get a show canceled.

"Oh man, someone was angry enough to search out a Samuel L. Jackson stupid-ass-decision gif."

Etta snorted. "Aging but good. It applies to so much in life."

Remy gave a chuckle and agreed.

Ash tightened his lips.

"Oooh, look." Remy leaned toward him, and Ash finally looked up.

The screen had a picture of someone sobbing and eating ice cream. Despite himself, Ash read the text underneath: *tfw you discover you're never going to see Niamish come to fruition.*

Ash stared. He wanted to feel moved that this viewer cared, but....

"They hate us."

"Huh?" Remy pulled the phone back and frowned at the screen.

"Naw, no'—how can you.... They hate enough to get us canceled. Ah dinnae...." Ash huffed and looked down at his book. "How can you even—" Ash shrugged and didn't finish the thought.

"Because the fans' outrage helps make it better? I get that some people were dipshits with the complaining, but the people who aren't, the ones who like us, they're being louder right now. And *that* gives me hope." Remy reached out and tangled their fingers together. "The world is always gonna suck, which is why you gotta give more energy to the less sucky parts."

Ash looked at their hands and the way Remy's slim darker fingers curled snugly against his own—so different and yet a perfect match. When he lifted his head, Remy met his gaze unflinchingly. Ash leaned forward and kissed him, slow and sweet.

**LIFE** fell into a new routine after that. Remy stayed over more nights than not, given neither of them had anywhere pressing to be most days and Remy's dog-walking clients lived closer to Ash.

Ash could take a few weeks to mourn before trying to find a new gig. He only wished Remy could do the same.

Remy asked his few clients to send any other pet owners his way and then began to search job sites in earnest. He spent too much time sitting on Ash's couch, staring at his computer screen, and chewing on his lower lip.

Remy glanced up, caught Ash staring, and said, "Stop being a creeper and tell me if I should apply to these people."

Ash rolled his eyes and settled closer to see the screen. "A temp agency?"

Remy blew out a loud breath. "Yeah I know. But at least I would be making some money."

"You know," Ash said awkwardly, "if you ever need a-a loan—"

Remy shook his head. "I wouldn't want to—but thank you. That you're offering means a lot."

Ash titled his head. "Okay. Um, obviously I'm offering because I fancy you a wee bit, but...." He blew out a breath. "You do know I'm comfortable enough to give any mate a hand, aye?"

Remy stared at him, then leaned forward to plant a hard, passionate kiss to his mouth.

"Um." Ash licked his lips. His trousers were growing tight. "What was that for?"

"For wanting to look after me, even if I clearly can't let you. Now shut up and tell me if you think I should apply to this agency."

"If I shut up, how can I—"

Remy shoved a hand in his face and pushed him away, then slipped it down to his shoulder and pulled him back. "*Numpty*," he said with such fondness Ash's insides melted. He wasn't sure what his face did, but Remy turned pink and leaned in for another kiss. At least, Ash thought, as he slid his hands up Remy's shirt, he still had this.

**JULY** passed by in an unemployed haze and came to a close. The hot dry summer days stretched into August, and Ash admitted to Etta that maybe, four weeks on, it was time to consider letting his agent send him new scripts.

He didn't email her.

Instead he went for another run and skipped the gym, again, to avoid weight training. Motivation to keep up the Hamish physique—in shape but not hulking— had died. At least the running—and the long nights with Remy in bed—would keep him from gaining fifty pounds from all the ice-cream binges.

He stuck to a familiar route, headed south to loop round Queen Elizabeth Park, and got home a few hours later, tired and boggin. Then he laid out his yoga mat and stretched until he'd cooled down enough to take a shower.

Dressed in old jeans and a lightweight hoodie, Ash was chopping vegetables for an omelet when Remy arrived.

"Hey, you," Remy said sweetly and leaned in for a slow snog. Ash gripped the knife tightly and pinned his knuckles to the counter. He didn't want to forget about the blade while under the tease of Remy's tongue.

"'Lo," Ash murmured against his mouth. Remy huffed a laugh, and the puff of air tingled against Ash's wet lips.

"Dork." He pressed a quick, closed-mouthed kiss to Ash's lips and pulled away. "What are you making me for lunch?"

Ash snorted. "I thought I'd show off my omelet skills, now that you have me trained."

Remy hummed. "I do, don't I." He waggled his eyebrows and gave Ash a once-over. His leer was reminiscent of the one he'd given Ash two nights ago when he pulled the antique cock ring out of his pocket with a guilty shrug. "So I forgot to gift it," he'd said not so innocently. Ash had thought wearing it might be embarrassing, but as he lay spent and exhausted over an hour later, *embarrassing* wasn't the word that came to mind.

Now, despite himself and the several rounds of sex they'd had over the past month, Ash blushed.

"Well." He cleared his throat. "Now I know what you like and have some practice, I figured I could show you."

"Mmm, Ash? How hungry are you?" Ash lifted his gaze; Remy watched him with dark eyes and lowered lashes. "Because I'm a bit peckish, but I'm really *hungry*."

Ash's stomach swooped with anticipation. "Lunch can wait," he said, surprised at how deep his voice sounded.

Remy shivered, grinned, and dragged Ash to his bedroom.

Later, after they were sated and curled up together, Remy picked the coin up off Ash's chest and smoothed it between his fingers. "I've never seen you without this."

Ash hummed.

"Can I ask about it? I mean, I see you touch it sometimes, under your shirt…."

"My da found it on the street, which was luck in itself, it's an old coin. But that night Maw told him she was pregnant again, so he figured it was the luckiest of coins and had it strung."

"Oh," Remy said softly.

"Da died when I was wee. Forgot to wear this that day." Ash reached down and picked the coin up, felt the familiar unicorn pattern beneath his thumb. "There was an accident." He cleared his throat. "Anyway, when I got older, Langston and Maw said I should have it. I dinnae remember him."

"I'm sorry," Remy whispered.

"No' your fault." He turned onto his side, settling face-to-face, and smiled. "Wearing it is like getting to know him. Besides, I wear it always, and I have you, so it must be lucky."

"Must be," Remy said softly and leaned in to kiss him. "I never knew my dad. Was just me and Mom, until Stepdad."

"I'm sorry," Ash whispered.

"Don't be. We were fine without him." He didn't sound bitter or sad, just honest. "Besides—Stepdad did all right."

Once their stomachs started growling, they got back into clothes and stumbled out to the kitchen on wobbly knees. Or at least Ash did. Remy's tongue always took some time to recover from.

They made quick work of the omelets and soon settled with them on the couch. Remy moaned over his and several times leaned in close to brush a thank-you kiss against Ash's cheek. "Best boyfriend ever," he murmured.

"I try," Ash said shyly. Contentment filled him, and he could almost forget the melancholy of the past month. "You know I'm grateful, yeah? This month sucked, but it sucked less with you." Even the prospect of a new job didn't seem daunting.

That earned him a lingering kiss.

"And I'm glad you made me listen to all those tweets about fans missing us." They had eased the hurt, eventually.

"Good." Remy ran his knuckles along Ash's jaw.

"And for helping me remember we still did good, even if it was a short run." Maybe he'd even have enough courage to try again, find another nonstraight role.

"Yeah, you did do good." He rested his hand around Ash's neck and swept his thumb back and forth. "It might be a silly fantasy show, but it's still important. And I'm proud of you for doing it, for helping others to see we're normal." He smiled tenderly.

Last year, in a restaurant, Remy had talked about being out. Ash recalled, as he had many times before, the fierceness in Remy's gaze, the passion in his words. The memory had shamed him in the past, but pride and satisfaction welled up in him now.

He swallowed. "Thank you. And you did it too, you know."

"Yeah. Helping to fight the bigots, you and me."

"Aye. Regular superheroes, us." Ash nodded seriously.

"Oh yeah." Remy smiled and ran his hand down to Ash's shoulder. "I look great in spandex."

Ash laughed. "What, no ripped gloves and trench coat like your namesake?"

Remy squawked and shoved Ash away. Chuckling, Ash straightened and tried to move in for a kiss, but Remy shoved a pillow in his face.

With a growl, Ash pushed it away and pounced. Using moves Etta had taught him, he pinned a wriggling Remy beneath him. Ash cupped one hand around Remy's face and ran his thumb across his cheekbone. "And," he said softly, "I can never regret *Mythfits*. It brought you back into my life."

"Wow," Remy murmured, his laughter calming, though the flush remained on his cheeks. He shifted and pulled Ash closer. "That was the most romantic and cornball thing anyone has ever said to me."

Ash's cheeks burned, but he pushed on. "It's true. I regretted not getting your number the moment you left."

"Yeah?" Remy's nose scrunched under the force of his grin. "Ashland Wells, were you pining after me?"

Ash looked down, the shyness not entirely an act. "Well, you *did* shove your face into my crotch...."

"Oh my God. I can't believe—I thought we were never mentioning that," Remy yelped.

Ash grinned. "Well, it was super memorable."

Remy smacked his shoulder. "Ugh. That's one word for it. Such an idiot." He paused and considered Ash. "Though... you were a gentleman about it." Ash preened. "Until now. Bringing it up, you great big jerk."

Ash laughed and reeled his boyfriend in for a kiss.

They cuddled on the couch, their movements slow and lazy, tangled up together, touching for the sake of touching, gently running their hands over each other's body, on top of clothes.

Ash had slipped his hand under Remy's shirt and rested it against the small of his back to palm his warm skin, when his phone rang.

He pulled away and blinked with surprise. "That's Janet's ringtone."

Remy stared back with equal shock. "You better answer it. What if she's got a new project?"

"That could be good," Ash said without hesitation. He reached toward the coffee table.

"Hello?"

"Ashland." Janet sounded surprisingly upbeat. "How are you?"

"Fine," he said, caution catching his tongue.

"Great. I got some news."

He listened as she spoke and responded only to agree and say goodbye.

"Well? What did she say?" Remy tapped an impatient staccato on Ash's thigh.

"She says the producers have been talking to Netflix." Ash ruminated over that one. *Netflix.* "They bought *Mythfits*. We're going to finish the season."

## Chapter Fourteen

**"HAMISH!"** Jasmine jumped into Ash's arms, and Ash embraced the hug. Why exactly had he avoided Jasmine for those few *Mythfits*-less weeks?

Jasmine hopped down, grinning ear to ear. "Can you believe it?"

"Naw, I cannae believe it." He shook his head and grinned back.

"Darling! Sugarplum!" Michael swanned into the room, followed more sedately by Kim, who was rolling her eyes. More hugs were shared, and Michael, the jerk, planted a smacking kiss to Ash's forehead. Lastly Miya made her entrance, and the group was complete. Energy buzzed between them. Even Kim displayed her excitement and lifted Miya right off her feet when they hugged.

Janet called them to order, and like giggling schoolchildren, they settled around the table.

"I can't tell you how lovely it is to see you." She beamed. "The producers have been hashing this out for weeks, almost from the moment news broke about us being canceled, and I wanted so bad to tell all of you, but I didn't want to get your hopes up. And, you know, I didn't want to get sued." Her grin turned wry, and they chuckled. "But we're here now, rescued by Netflix—who paid a whole whack of money to get us—and the good news keeps coming. First, that episode that got trashed? Netflix wants to add it to the season, on top of the other thirteen filmed or planned." They cheered. She lifted her phone and waggled it about. "Second, I received an email this morning. 'Dear Ms. Hum, we are delighted to inform you we successfully booked slots for your show at Seattle Comic-Con.'"

Jasmine whooped with delight, and Miya squeaked into her hands, her eyes wide. Michael tossed his head back and laughed. Kim's eyes widened and she muttered, "No way."

Ash sat still, an eejit's grin plastered on his face. Seattle Con was one of the largest in the US, and the second biggest on the west coast.

Janet raised her voice. "What can I say? Netflix really believes in us. Of course there are details to iron out with your respective people, but all five of you are invited. Keep your calendars clear for August, folks, because we're going to Washington." She winked and sat down, and the five of them broke into applause.

Damn, it was good to be back.

**REMY** was back on salary too, which meant more breathing room for him. Ash couldn't stop grinning after Remy called to confirm his reinstatement.

"Netflix is already talking about season two, and Janet mentioned my script again."

"That's fab. That—" Ash floundered. "I'm so chuffed for you," he said at last, softer.

"Yeah." Remy's voice went soft too, and Ash pictured him sitting at home in his living room, maybe curled up in his pajamas and looking invitingly cozy on the couch. If only Ash could join him.

A week later—and a few times in between—Ash and Remy *were* curled up together on Ash's couch and watching *Cake Wars* when Adele sent a flurry of texts.

*Halloooooooooooo!*

*Guess what!*

*Guess who's coming back to Vanny!!*

*This guy!*

Attached to the last text was a gif of herself in character saying "I'm back, ladies"—*ladies* being Moira's favorite mass noun for her friends.

Ash rolled his eyes and texted back, *How come?*

She called him, of course.

"We just got everything all confirmed, and I'm guest starring on your show. Apparently I'm gonna play your boyfriend's ex."

For one disorienting moment, Ash thought, *But Remy's not on the show.* Then reality reasserted. "They're not dating yet."

"Yeah, I guess that's where I come in," she said happily.

Ash snorted. "When do you fly in?"

"Wednesday night. Scheduling issues, but they really wanted your former flame for this one. Also, hells yes I want to play a fairy. Anyway, gonna call in to the table read on Monday. Then I'm going to see my boo on Thursday."

"Uh-huh." Ash chuckled.

"Oh, and I'm not flying out until Saturday afternoon, so you're mine on Friday night, right?"

"Right." He couldn't have kept the smile from his voice even if he wanted to.

Remy arched a brow at him after he hung up the phone.

"Adele. She says she's playing Niall's ex. It'll be good to see her."

"You've missed her a lot."

"Yeah. She's one of my closest friends."

"Well, I can't wait to meet her." Remy took his hand, slotted their fingers together.

"You'll love her."

"The Grace to your Will." Remy frowned. "No, that would be Etta…. The Karen to your Jack?"

Ash blinked. "Er, more like, aye. But she doesn't know, um, about me."

"Oh." Remy froze, apparently taking this in.

"I just never—I mean, I've never really told anyone but Etta and Langston."

"Ah. Okay. Good to know." He cleared his throat and shook his head. Then he tilted it to the side. "You know, the ex-girlfriend's description matches Adele's, in the script."

Relieved, Ash snorted. "Of course it does. Also, way to warn me about my 'boyfriend's' ex showing up." He gave Remy's bicep a light pinch. Remy squirmed away from the touch and burrowed in closer under Ash's arm.

"And lose my job? For you?" He smirked, but there was something—"I mean the sex is good, but I'm not sure it's that good." He lifted his eyebrows in apparent invitation.

Ash accepted. He wrapped his arm more securely around Remy's shoulder and flipped him onto his back. Using his greater body mass, he pressed Remy into the couch and murmured, "I'll show you good."

"Hmm," Remy hummed in agreement. "I sure hope so."


**ASH** had missed working with Adele.

Thursday felt like old times. She arrived on set, larger than life, and proceeded to dazzle everyone with good looks and charm. "No one can resist this golden face," she said cheekily when Ash teased her. At lunch she held court, gathered everyone around and told stories, especially embarrassing ones about Ash.

The plot for the episode was much like she'd said— Niall's ex comes to town and stirs things up. Janet said it would bear fruit in the finale, as she wanted to have minor emotional cliffhangers for all the characters, and there was really only one thing to focus on for Hamish and Niall.

The two days filming with Adele flew past, and soon he and Adele were headed out for dinner on Friday.

*Dinner tonight?* Remy had texted around four.

Ash replied, *Sorry. :( Dinner with Addy.* Then he got back to work.

He didn't see the response until much later, when Adele headed to the bathroom midmeal.

*K. See you tomorrow.*

He smiled at the assumption that they would see each other soon and was contemplating his reply when Adele landed back in her seat with an *oof.* He slid the phone into his pocket and asked, "You alright?"

"Peachy. I'm not that drunk. But I *am* getting old."
She sighed. "Can you believe I turned thirty-two?"

He shook his head. It was hard to believe they'd
met for the first time seven years earlier. God, they'd
been babies then. "We met a lifetime ago."

"Yes. Those were the days, when I was young
and naïve, convinced this Hollywood gig was easy."
*Restraint* was not only her first big paid role but also
one of the first auditions she'd done for TV.

He shook his head. "Tell me about it."

"Here's to us—older, wiser, and better." She held
up her pint glass, and they knocked them together.

"Don't let this be our last visit together this trip,"
she said after calling for a taxi. She tilted her head. "Tell
me you're free for brunch. I'm going to need greasy
bacon and carbs tomorrow."

He smiled. He'd probably want the same. "Come
over for eleven, and I'll serve you a spread, show off
my new cooking skills."

"Damn. You're on. See you tomorrow." She leaned
in and pressed a kiss to his cheek, and then she was in
the car and gone.


**SHE** got to his place at half eleven, which he should
have expected. On the upside, it meant everything was
prepped and waiting for him to cook and she missed the
minor catastrophe at five after when he almost cut off
his finger and broke a glass.

She watched him over her coffee, still beautiful
despite her obvious hangover. Even her copper skin
and green eyes weren't dimmed by the somewhat pallid
undertones from last night. She eyed him suspiciously and
made judgmental sounds at his toaster. "It doesn't 'pop.'"

"It beeps instead."

"It's unnatural."

He rolled his eyes, threw the toast on the plates, and served her. "Don't look a gift breakfast in the mouth. Now drink your coffee and eat."

"Bossy," she mumbled and then dug in.

They were giggling over cleaned plates and munching on the last of the bacon when a knock came at the door.

Frowning, Ash answered it.

*Why is Remy—oh. Shit.* Ash glanced at the clock and guilt burned in his belly. Remy had promised to come over for lunch and show him how to make risotto because Ash had mentioned how much he liked it. Bugger.

"Hey," Remy said, smiling and carrying grocery bags. Buggering shite. He stepped in close, and Ash shuffled back into the flat.

"You remember Adele?" They'd met briefly on set, but Remy hadn't been able to join them for lunches.

"Huh? Oh." Remy blinked several times as he took in the scene. Then, after ages, he smiled again. It looked... weird. "How nice to see you."

He brought his groceries to the kitchen and set them down. "Catching up?"

"Before I fly out. It's Ray, right?"

The smile dimmed a fraction. "Remy."

"Right, of course! I'm sorry, not my strong suit, names."

"No problem."

"So, what brings you here?" Adele asked, looking at the bags.

"Oh, cooking class."

"Remy's been teaching me," Ash blurted.

"O-ho. He discovered your Jamie Oliver obsession, did he?"

Remy kept smiling that weird smile. "Maybe."

"He's a fantastic cook." Ash shifted his weight. "I helped him get to know the city, he offered lessons in return."

"Well, brunch this morning was delicious. Good job, kid," she said and patted her stomach.

There was a flicker in Remy's eyes, but it quickly disappeared. He shrugged. "Oh, you know. I gotta eat." The smile was nothing like the one he always gave Ash—heat curled in his belly at the distracting realization. Remy had an "Ash" smile.

"Well, I'm glad you're so generous. I'm well fed, and I guess you're to thank." She looked at the clock and groaned. "And it's about time I got ready to hit the road. Flight's outbound in three hours, and I still have to make it to the airport." She stood and sighed. "I'm gonna hit the head and then say goodbye." She ambled off.

Ash began to tidy up the dishes.

"She seems nice."

"She is." Ash bit his lip, then decided it better to confess sooner than later. "I'm sorry. I forgot about lunch today. I guess the excitement of seeing her made me a bit of a dunderheid, huh?"

Remy scanned his face, then said, "Okay. Understandable I guess. Forgive you." He tipped up and pressed a kiss to Ash's cheek.

"Thanks." The bathroom door opened, and Ash stepped away. He put the dishes in the dishwasher.

"Well, it's been fabulous to see you, darling." Adele held out her arms and they embraced. "It was too long. Let's not do that again, okay?"

"Nope."

"Remy, it was good to meet you again." She gave him a hug, which surprised Remy, judging by the awkward stiffness of his motions.

"You too."

She patted his chest and then found her purse and slung it over her shoulder. "One more hug for the road, boo." She hugged him tight and he did likewise. Then she pressed a kiss to his lips. "Tickles," she said, stroking his beard. "Still the hottest, though."

Shaking his head and laughing, he said by rote, "You're still hotter."

"Damn right I am." She smacked her butt, smacked his, and then left with one last "Toodles!"

Ash shook his head again and closed the door.

"Well. She's... interesting," Remy said dryly.

"That's one word for it."

"You had a good visit?"

"Really good. Didn't realize how much I missed her. We were in each other's pockets for about ten months of the year for six years."

"Yeah. She knows you pretty well, I guess."

Ash nodded.

Remy looked at him, chewing his lip, then apparently came to a decision. "But she doesn't know you're gay."

Ash froze in the middle of emptying one of the grocery bags. "No." He cleared his throat. "No one knows that."

"Right." Remy licked his lips and thought for a moment. Then he looked up at Ash and smiled—and *there* was the good smile back again. "So I'm guessing you're not up for lunch." He looked at the dirty dishes and smirked. Ash knew where this was going. "Wanna cuddle on the couch with a movie?"

All right, not the bed suggestion he predicted, but almost as good. "Definitely."

**ASH** slept in the next morning, and when he finally pulled out of sleep, he found the bed half-empty.

Etta's bedroom door was shut tight—not surprising considering her long day at a competition yesterday—and Remy was sat at the window between the built-ins, arms wrapped around his knees as he stared out at the city.

"Mornin'," Ash said and made for the kettle. Remy didn't move. Frowning, Ash changed course and headed for him. "Morning."

"Hmm?" Remy turned and blinked at him.

"Good morning." Ash swiped a thumb along Remy's cheekbone. "Deep thoughts?"

Remy shrugged. The usual animation in his body slowly returned, and he offered a smile. "Maybe. Woke up too early this morning." He shook himself. Ash sat at his feet, taking the rest of the bench.

"Something the matter?"

Remy's eyes flickered, but he shook his head. "Nope."

Uncertain if that was the truth but figuring he could do little about it until Remy opted to tell him, Ash nodded and pressed a kiss to Remy's forehead. "Well. I'm here if you want to chat. Until then, shall we make some breakfast?"

"Yeah. Yeah, let's do that."

They worked well in the kitchen, and with each meal, they only got better at sharing the space, divvying up work. That morning they made it through the whole process without once colliding.

Etta found them some time later sitting at the breakfast bar and reading.

"Well," she said, after she'd made herself tea. "Aren't you two disgustingly cute."

"Yeah. Cute, that's us," Remy agreed, but his tone had a flatness.... Surely being cute wasn't a bad thing?

"Cutest." Ash kissed his temple.

Remy gave a wee smile, then turned off his phone and said, "It's getting late. I should go if I want to run all my errands." Remy hadn't said anything about having errands today, and certainly not so much as to consider half nine as "late."

"Okay."

Remy squeezed his hand and left to get ready.

Ash watched him go, a frown tugging at his brow. When he turned back, Etta was staring at him.

"He okay?"

Ash shook his head. "He says yes."

She hummed somewhat doubtfully and took a long drink of her tea. Then she also left to clean up.

Ash rose and tidied the kitchen, but worry niggled in the back of his mind.

Yesterday hadn't exactly gone smoothly, what with Ash screwing up his schedule and the strained meeting between Remy and Adele. Ash didn't think Remy held a grudge over a bit of forgetfulness. After all, Remy had forgotten a date or two himself. But he couldn't deny Remy had been bothered by the meeting.

*Probably because you introduced him as a friend*, said a very reasonable part of his brain.

Ash shied away from the idea. Remy had always known how things would be.

*But he asked you—*

Ash turned away. He rinsed the dishes and put them in the dishwasher.

They hadn't done much at all after Adele left. Remy had been quieter than usual, but not especially so.

He put the ketchup in the fridge and thought about the lack of sex. Again, not unusual.

He was washing the frying pans when Remy came out of the bedroom, clean and dressed. He wore last night's skinny jeans, a fresh long-sleeve tee, and a scarf with… Wonder Woman on it. Ash smiled.

Remy pushed his sleeves up and gathered all his belongings. He threw his notebook into his already-stuffed messenger bag holding yesterday's outfit, and slung it over his shoulder. "Right."

Ash dried off his hands and met Remy at the door. "Have a good day."

"You too."

Ash leaned forward and pressed a kiss to his mouth. To his surprise, Remy leaned up and returned it with fervor, snogging Ash with passion, as if they'd never snogged before. Or maybe, like they never would again. When Remy pulled back, they were panting and Remy's lips were wet and shining.

"Well, I guess I better…."

"Okay." Ash blinked several times. "See you tomorrow."

"Yeah. Tomorrow." Remy smiled and left.

Ash hoped whatever was bothering Remy sorted itself out soon.


**ON** Monday, Ash could barely contain the nervous butterflies in his stomach as he settled in for the table read. Still on edge from the uncertain way he and Remy had left things the day before, he could hardly believe he was readying himself for this finale.

"Are you nervous about it?" Remy had asked Saturday night.

"Why would I be?"

"You're going to be kissing a man in public for the first time."

Ash considered it and then shrugged. "Yeah, but it's not real. It's pretend." No one was going to draw any conclusions. Besides, the kiss would be short. They'd do several takes, but the script called for a short, closed-mouthed thing.

"Right." Remy frowned thoughtfully.

Then a thought struck Ash. "You're not worried about it, are you? Me snogging someone else."

"No," Remy said. "I'm not worried about you 'snogging someone else.' I know it's not really you and Michael kissing. I told you I'm not jealous of him."

"Good. Because I'd never pick snogging Michael over you." He leaned in and kissed the tip of Remy's nose.

"Dork," Remy said and smiled. Ash thought he saw a shadow in his eyes—had he not been truthful?— but he hoped it was his imagination.

Ash pushed the memory away. He had a table read to get through.

When they reached The Moment, Michael leaned over and smacked a very loud and wet kiss to Ash's cheek. The rest of the cast jeered and catcalled.

And even though it was fake and platonic, Ash's heart beat double time at the ruse—hiding his gay in plain sight.

"Thank you, darling," he said lightly and wiped his cheek, unable to repress a grin.

The grin didn't last.

Once they finished the read, he headed off in search of Remy and found him sat by himself in the writers' office with his headphones in and staring, once again, out a window.

Ash lifted a hand to knock just as Remy said, "Yeah, I don't know. I'm not sure what to think or say."

Oh, the phone.

Feeling awkward, he resumed his knock. Remy jerked and turned.

"Hey. What? Sorry, Nisha. Ash walked in. Talk to you later? … Okay, love you too. Bye."

When Remy pulled the buds from his ears, Ash said, "Hello." He didn't know what else to say, and he felt awkward like he hadn't been since Remy moved here.

"What's up?" Remy asked, faux casual.

Ash cringed. He'd never heard that tone before Saturday, but he was already sick of it. "I came to check on you."

For a long time, Remy stared out the window, and Ash waited for him. At last Remy sighed and turned back to him. "We should have a chat."

"Right." Ash swallowed. "I'm done for the day, if you want…?"

"Sure. I should finish up here, but…."

"Dinner? I'll cook?"

Remy smiled, a small but genuine thing. "I'd like that."

"Good."

"Yeah."

"Well. I guess I better—" Ash motioned toward the doorway.

"Yeah. I'll, uh, see you later."

"Later," Ash said and headed out.

The dread still sat heavy in his stomach and grew worse at the soft sound of Remy's quiet "Bye."

**ETTA** brought Ash home, asked if he'd be all right by himself, and left for her afternoon class.

Ash took a look through the kitchen and settled on making the chicken pasta thing Remy had taught him. But he wouldn't need to start for some time yet.

So he sat in the bay window with a cup of tea, sipped slowly at it, and fretted.

At four he forced himself out of his seat and prepared dinner. Remy didn't buzz at the door until almost half six, late even by Remy's standards.

He smiled and greeted Ash with a sweet hello and a lingering snog, but there was a somberness to his expression and a desperateness to the kiss. Alarm spread in Ash's belly.

"Hi. Are you hungry?" Ash asked, hoping to put off whatever conversation Remy thought they needed to have. Suddenly he desperately didn't want to know.

"Sure. I can always eat. You know that."

Dinner was awful, their easy manner gone.

"Did you have a good day?" Ash tried in desperation.

"Hmm? Oh, yes. Fine."

"Good… good…."

By the time dinner ended, Ash figured maybe he did want to force the conversation after all. Anything had to be better than this parody of intimacy.

He opened his mouth just as Remy asked, "Are you happy?"

"What?"

Remy shook his head. "No, that's not… I mean—" He sighed. "Do you think you'll ever come out?"

Ash stared. "Come out?"

"Yeah. Let strangers know you're gay."

Ash thought of Sam, a career dead in the water. "No."

"Right." Remy looked down at his mostly empty plate and pushed the remnants around with his fork. "I got an email from my thesis advisor. He got a grant and is setting up a program at McGill—in Montreal. He'll need an assistant, and he's offered me the job."

Ice filled Ash's veins. "What?" he croaked.

"I mean, it's not something I went looking for, okay? But I got it the other day and—I mean, it's the first job offer for something approaching stable that I've had, and maybe it's a sign, you know?"

Ash didn't know. In fact, he was totally at sea. "Of what?"

Remy sighed, and his eyes filled with that damnable shadow. "That we're not meant to be."

Ash clutched at the counter. He didn't understand what was happening. He thought they were good together, excellent even, and—didn't Remy think likewise?

Remy sighed and rubbed a hand through his hair. "Look, I like you, Ash. I like you really a lot and I like being with you but… I've been kidding myself thinking it didn't matter if you weren't out or that we didn't need to worry about it, but it does and we do." He sighed, and the coldness reached Ash's stomach. "When it was just not holding hands in public, it didn't seem like a big deal, you know? And running around to find secluded corners was fun." He gave a tiny smile. "It was kind of thrilling to make out in my office." His smile died. "But avoiding PDAs is one thing. Not telling our friends… I can't do that. I can't meet one of your oldest friends and have you sit there and tell her nothing, to lie about who I am. I need—need to be important to someone."

He lifted his head and turned pleading eyes on Ash. "I need you to understand this, okay? Because, God, I wish, I really wish I was the kind of person who could live in secrecy. But I can't, Ash. I need openness. I need to not live a life where I have to remember which friends know about us and which don't. Where I'm not wondering if this time he's gonna love me enough to tell 'em." A sharp cold pain stabbed Ash in the gut, and his mouth was dry. Remy took a deep breath. "So maybe we're not meant to be, and maybe this job is a sign and I should go." He swallowed and stood. Then he leaned forward and gently kissed Ash on the forehead and then the mouth. "I'm sorry," he whispered. And he left.

Ash sat, frozen, his limbs numb, and stared into space.

Etta found him several minutes later and let out a soft noise of surprise. "Ash? Are you okay?" She reached out and ran a thumb over his cheek. "Are you... crying?"

"I think," he said, his voice rusty, "I just got dumped." He turned to Etta.

Her eyes were wide, and she let out a soft, surprised "Oh."

"And it really hurts," he whispered, and she wrapped her arms around him in a tight embrace and didn't let go.

## *Chapter Fifteen*

**THE** week crawled by.

As much as Ash would have liked to stay in bed for the duration, he had a job that needed doing. So every morning he put on his happy face and went to work.

They filmed The Scene on Friday.

Ash's hands shook before the first take, and not just from a lack of sleep. His stomach was a jumble of nerves, but when the director called action and he slipped into Hamish and Michael into Niall and they started ranting at each other, it felt easy.

Michael missed a mark, and they cut. Ash shook himself and took a moment.

Michael made his mark the next time, and soon they were standing opposite each other and shouting— until Michael gripped his face and planted a hard, eager kiss to Ash's mouth. The first touch of non-Remy male lips ever—the first since the breakup. *Not now.*

After the four beats passed, they pulled away from each other and stood gaping until the director shouted, "Cut."

Michael snorted and giggled. His hands, still framing Ash's face, began to shake. Sometimes when filming, all the tension built up and released in a fit of uncontrollable laughter. Which could be highly contagious. And Ash, who'd been running on little sleep and shoving his broken heart away, grabbed hold of the fit of hysterics like a lifeline. Soon they were giggling like lads, holding on to each other. Ash gasped, near desperate for breath.

"I'm sorry," Michael said. He wiped his face. "I don' know what—it's just, your face."

"Gee, thanks," Ash sputtered.

"Nah. Only, you went cross-eyed, darlin'. You looked adorable." He bopped Ash on the nose.

Ash batted his hand away. "Ye numpty. Hamish were looking at Niall's daft face." He pressed a hand into said face and pushed it away.

The director cleared his throat. "Boys, if you're ready, we'll do another take?"

Chastened, they nodded and agreed. As they moved to find their places, Ash caught sight of Remy standing on the sidelines.

The joy he'd managed to wrangle for a minute died, leaving an empty hollow in its place.

Remy gave a curt nod and then turned and walked off the soundstage. For the second time that week, he left Ash behind—bereft, hurt, and lonely.

## *Chapter Sixteen*

**OVER** the next few days, without work to distract him, Ash felt like he was living in a dream. He'd never got the breakup songs and montages before, but he now understood the desire to lie on the floor and listen to Adele or Natalie Imbruglia on repeat.

Etta bought him ice cream, and the first day post-shooting, they each ate a Ben and Jerry's pint while watching Batman cartoons.

"I'm sorry," she said during the doomed love story of Mr. Freeze. "I know you really like him."

"Thank you," he said later, after Batman watched Catwoman leave him once again.

The thing was, the breakup—he swallowed hard at the word—had blindsided him, which was moronic. It should have been obvious they couldn't go on in secret.

Hadn't Remy told him that very first day that he was out and proud for a reason?

He shouldn't have been surprised, but he had been. He hadn't expected Remy to tell him he'd reached his breaking point. Had there been warning signs before Adele's visit?

Ash couldn't recall any, but that didn't mean there hadn't been. Probably he'd been too happy, too... in love to notice anything the matter.

On Tuesday he cleaned the kitchen top to bottom, emptying drawers and cupboards to scrub them down. He remembered how his maw used to clean when she was upset. She'd done the whole house top to bottom after Ash's grandfather had died. Pushing away thoughts of her—he was sad enough without thinking about the mother he'd lost fourteen years ago—Ash tried to focus on the issue at hand. His dirty kitchen.

He wished he still had work to distract him, but until they left for Comic-Con Thursday afternoon, his schedule was wide-open. He had nothing to do but think about the doomed nature of his relationship—ex-relationship. He and Remy could never be together as long as Remy wanted to be out and Ash needed to hide. Stalemate unless something changed. And it wouldn't be Remy's mind.

*Nor should it.* Ash scrubbed harder at the grease. The thought of asking him to....

God, he'd been a blind eejit, a right dunderheid.

Ash tended to overthink. Unlike Remy, he wasn't good at jumping in feetfirst and trusting he'd learn to swim. Getting caught flat-footed because he hadn't tortured himself with doomsday scenarios was new for him. Lessoned learned.

By the time he and Etta drove out two days later, Ash was knackered, sore, and grumpy. Etta narrowed her eyes at him and sighed noisily about what a joy he'd be to travel with. She relented a bit when he gave her the puppy-dog eyes, and she flung a sleeping mask at him as she settled behind the wheel. If only he *could* sleep.

**ASH'S** alarm went off way too early on Friday morning. He'd had dinner with his castmates and their traveling partners the night before, while he did his best to pretend he was fine.

They had interviews in the morning, and in the afternoon a full-cast panel in one of the main halls.

Ash hoped it wasn't embarrassingly empty.

The day started with a relay marathon. The *Mythfits* bigwigs paired him and Michael together, of course, and the ladies as a second group, and they spent the morning rotating between media outlets, answering the same questions over and over.

Thank God Michael was not only good at this but actually enjoyed it. Ash didn't possess the energy to brave it alone.

"What attracted you to the role?" asked their current interviewer. Susie was kind and had done an admirable job setting the tone for their fifteen minutes together.

Michael grinned and gave the same response he'd given the others. "It was funny and different. Not a lot of comedy roles for black men that involve this kind of openness about their sexuality, especially a nonhetero one. Niall breaks a lot of stereotypes. If he wants to dance in a tutu, he'll do it and won't think twice about it. It's pretty freeing as an actor."

"Exactly," Ash said, giving her the sound bite he knew she wanted. "It's not often an ensemble cast has only one white man or fewer straight than queer characters. It's so much fun to be part of a project like that." He shrugged. "I won't pretend being white and male is tough, but all roles are limited in some way by stereotypes. It's fun for me to have the opportunity to play someone sweet and sensitive."

After Susie thanked them and they were hustled on their way, Michael leaned in and whispered, "We're getting good at answering that one, mate."

Ash snorted. They'd definitely done a good job of memorizing the answer and saying it over and over again.

Every time, it tasted of lies, heavy on his tongue.

Ash shoved that thought away. They had another interview.

By the time they broke for lunch, Ash wanted to call it a day—to curl up in bed, pull the duvet over himself, and hide for a week. Fortunately Michael seemed to view his increasing taciturnity as a challenge rather than an annoyance.

"Hang in there, mucker. Only one more interview for the day." He happily ate a pudding cup.

Ash didn't have the energy to eat dessert. He gave him a silent mulish look. "Right."

Etta chuckled and eyed them both with amusement from her seat across from them. "You're assuming the autograph lines are easier to deal with."

"Aren't they?" Michael's tone was genuine, so Ash didn't snap his head off.

He sighed. "Yes and no. Fans are nicer to talk to because at least they give a crap, but there's more of them and they're more unpredictable." Ash leaned his forehead on Michael's shoulder and sighed. "Thanks for covering my arse today."

Michael laughed. "No worries. It's such a lovely bum I couldn't resist. And don't worry. I'll sit next to you in the autograph line."

Ash lifted his head and gave him a weak smile, grateful for the offer, even if it probably wouldn't help.

Their panel was at two, and by the time the clock rolled around, Ash realized the bubbling in his stomach was eagerness, not dread. It probably helped that his castmates were all excited and vibrating with it.

When they walked on stage, one by one, he got the loudest cheers—being the most famous cast member—but not by much. Jasmine, Kim, and Miya all looked stunned by the volume raised in their honor.

Their host, Tom, was competent, and he asked a few general questions about the project and their characters. Then he threw it open to the fans.

The first few were mostly as expected. One guest wanted to know who was the funniest, another asked how Ash felt going from werewolf to brownie, and another what their favorite episodes were.

Then came the adorable kid. "Hi, I'm Toni" had buzzed hair, wore thick-framed glasses, a checked shirt, jeans, and rainbow suspenders, and looked no more than seventeen. She blushed as she stood in front of the camera and stuttered out, "It's so amazing seeing all these queer characters. My girlfriend and I were so excited. Especially to see two characters so openly bi. Thank you."

The cast nodded encouragingly, and Jasmine said, "I know, right?" The crowd cheered.

When the noise died down, Toni asked, "I wondered what you thought about that before you decided to play the roles."

Jasmine, smiling kindly, said, "Like, is that why we took the job? I think I speak for all of us when I say Hell. Yes."

The crowd cheered, and the girl glowed. Ash stared at her smiling pink face. A peace settled over him. They had done that. *He* had done that.

"It's so great to see a script take representation as a challenge. How many different groups can we get into one show?" Jasmine's grin turned wicked. "Also, how could I resist playing the brooding vamp all the girls swoon for." She winked to more cheers and applause.

Toni leaned to the mic and said, "Thank you."

And that would have been it. But Ash had the mic to his lips and was saying, "No, thank you," before he could even think about it.

Toni jerked and stared at him wide-eyed. He smiled; he hadn't meant to surprise her.

He cleared his throat. "You know, I took time off after *Restraint* finished, and I read a lot of scripts and said no to all of them. I didn't know what I was waiting for until I got *Mythfits*." He swallowed and kept his gaze on the girl, pretending it was only the two of them, though he felt surprisingly at ease. "When I read it, I knew I had to do it. Because I knew how much it would mean to people, how much it meant to me. So thank you for telling me it's worth it." He licked his lips. "Representation matters, and when you don't have any... you think you're strange and broken. I never could have told a roomful of strangers I was gay at your age. I couldn't have done it last week even." The room felt still, like all the air had been sucked out of it, but

Ash didn't take his eyes off the now very surprised girl. "Thank you." He blinked hard a few times, trying to will away the tears.

Michael and Miya, who were seated to either side of him, skootched closer and reached for him. She took his hand, and Michael squeezed his knee. The crowd clapped and cheered, a few hooted, but Ash didn't care, because Toni was beaming at him.

"You know," she said thoughtfully, "my girlfriend has always said if she ever left me for anyone, it would be you"—Ash blushed at the thought of breaking up a couple of *kids*—"so thanks for crushing the dream!" Then she rushed away from the mic as the crowd laughed.

"Breaking hearts," Michael said into his mic. "But I think, mate, you gave rise to a whole new set of dreams." He wiggled his eyebrows.

Ash took his hand back and hid his face in it.

"We won't tell them all he's taken, then," Kim said, deadpan.

The crowd laughed, and Ash jerked with surprise. She winked at him and… did she know?

A question for later—another fan was talking at the mic.

Ash sat back, breathed deep, and took the time to collect himself. He was probably already all over Twitter—with video too, he bet. By the time he got off the stage, his agent would be calling. Etta must be freaking out, if in a good way. But he didn't have to worry about the mayhem yet. Ash could simply sit and enjoy the moment and the memory of surprise and joy on the girl's face. He hoped she came to his autograph lineup later so he could thank her again.

## Chapter Seventeen

**ETTA** tackled him with a hug, his agent sighed and tutted down the line about "warnings, dammit!" and Remy sent him a single text. *Call me as soon as you can, please.*

His vision blurred as he stared at the phone clutched in his hand. That didn't sound very encouraging, and Ash wasn't certain he was ready to deal with it.

Besides, any conversation with Remy would take time, and he wouldn't have any of that until later. First he had several hours of autographs to work through.

Unsurprisingly, plenty of fans wanted to talk about Zvi, but Ash didn't mind. He would always love the character. But a gratifying number of people picked the promotional photo of Hamish and Niall and beamed at him as they told him how awesome he was for doing

*Mythfits* and for his honesty and how excited they were to hear Ash was "one of them."

*One of them.* He was one of them, part of a group, and not alone. Every single one of them teared him up, but he didn't cry, thank God—at least, not until he and Etta hid in their room.

As he sat down, the tears welled up and fell. Rapidly.

Etta wrapped her arms around him. "What's going on?"

He shook his head. "Nothing, nothing, am…. Shite." He sniffed. "Ah'm happy." He smiled at her.

Etta pulled away, laughed, and punched him in the arm. "Dick." She smiled at him. "I'm glad. About damned time."

It really, really was.

Etta shuffled off to order them some dinner.

The clock read barely half seven, early enough to call Remy.

He texted Langston a heads-up, despite it being the wee hours in Scotland—though he suspected the news had hit Twitter before bedtime in Glasgow.

He should call Remy. He had some apologies to deliver. But how could he do it over the phone? It was definitely not the right medium for saying certain things for the first time.

His stomach swooped. He couldn't believe he was debating the best way to tell Remy—

No. In person was better. He should put it off, tell Remy that their conversation would wait.

He settled on the couch with Etta, and after several long knee-jiggling moments, he gave in—to the pressure of Etta's hand on his knee and to the niggling in his gut—and texted Remy.

*I'm free now.*

He clutched his phone and waited for an answer. He stared blankly at the TV. Whatever was playing didn't help time pass faster.

A knock sounded on the door, and Etta poked him. "I gotta go to the bathroom, you answer."

Ash grumbled but accepted the distraction. Anything was better than ruminating on Remy and whether or not Ash could fix things, even fetching burgers from a bellhop.

He opened the door—and found Remy, wringing his hands, a frown marring his pretty features.

Ash's mouth dropped open and he stared. Remy was meant to be a border and a three-hour drive away.

"Please tell me you didn't just come out to the whole fucking world because of me," Remy said by way of hello, his voice tight and unhappy.

"I didn't come out to the whole bloody world because of you," he repeated numbly. Oh God, did Remy drive here after the panel? "What are you doing here?"

"I came for the con," he snapped and pushed into the room. Ash stumbled back, and they turned to face each other. Remy's unhappy frown had morphed into something thunderous. "Goddammit, Ash. This isn't a fucking joke," he snapped. "This isn't television, you can't come out as a romantic gesture. This is your life. People aren't going to fucking forget!"

"Hey," Ash mumbled. Did Remy think him that stupid? "Hey, numpty." Remy pressed his lips tight and fidgeted with the cuff of the hockey hoodie he wore for comfort. "No, I didnae come out for you." Ash took a deep breath. "I did it for me and only for me."

Remy stilled and looked Ash in the eye. "Yeah?"

"Aye." Ash cleared his throat and touched his pendant. "I've been doing a lot of thinking the past week. About what I want. I've no' been thinking lately, only… going along, assuming I felt like always."

"Oh." Remy's voice shook. "So if I'd waited or given you time…." His shoulders dropped, and his mouth downturned. He looked gutted.

"I prob'ly would have been an arse. I was an arse." Ash swallowed. "I'm sorry I didn't ever stop to think. You were right—"

"I wasn't any better. I—if I'd been thinking right, I never would have started dating you without bringing it up first. I guess I kind of got carried away in the romance of it all." Remy gave a weak chuckle and fussed with his cuff some more.

"No. I—I was worse. I got carried away and I didn't stop to even think about what I wanted anymore—"

Another knock sounded at the door, and Remy and Ash jumped.

"That would be room service," Etta called from the bedroom. And when had she moved there?

Etta emerged and headed for the door. Ash's feet were rooted to the carpet, and judging by Remy's wide eyes, he felt just as gobsmacked.

Etta accepted the room service and tipped the server. "Well, I'll leave you boys to it." She took a plate to her room and firmly shut the door.

Ash cleared his throat. "Why—you came for the con?"

Remy looked down and shifted awkwardly. "I bought the ticket weeks ago."

"Oh." Before everything went to shite. "But… why didn't you say anything?"

"Was gonna be a surprise," Remy mumbled. "So, surprise?"

"Ah. It's… it's a good surprise," Ash said round the lump in his throat.

"Yeah?" Remy's lips trembled. And were those tears?

"Aye."

Ash didn't know who moved first, but suddenly they were in each other's arms, clutching and grasping.

"I'm sorry," Ash whispered, his beard rasping against Remy's cheek and neck.

"Me too," Remy choked. Definitely tears.

"I know." Time for some truth. "You... you're all I want." He took a deep breath. "I love you," he whispered and closed his eyes. God, if Remy didn't say it back—

Remy pulled back enough to look into Ash's eyes. "Really?"

God, how could he doubt it? Ash had really buggered this up. "Of *course* I do. I love you so—"

Remy stoppered his words with a deep kiss. Ash returned it, tightening his arms, hardly daring to believe he was tasting that soft sweet mouth again.

And yet... Remy hadn't said it back. Ash's heart skipped a beat, and he kissed harder. If this was a last kiss, he would take all he could.

They parted, barely.

"I love you too," Remy breathed out, making Ash's heart beat double time. "So fucking much." He kissed Ash's jaw, his cheek. "It fucking killed me to walk away, but I knew... I was in so fucking deep already, and I couldn't—"

"I know," Ash soothed. He found it easier to sound calm now that buoying light bubbled through his chest. "I know. I was a dunderheid, remember? A right dafty walloper. We already went over this. I know." He ran his hands in gentle circles and bumped his nose to Remy's cheek.

Remy gave a shuddering sigh and snogged him dirtily. Ash shivered, but this couldn't wait.

"Remy, I know I don't deserve it, but I want tae ask you to-to—"

"Yes?"

"Take me back," he blurted. "I know I dinnae deserve it, deserve you. I well messed up." He licked his lips. "I hurt you when Adele came to visit, and I'm so sorry. Ever since, I've been wishing I'd told her the truth, called you my boyfriend. And I still want you to be—"

"Yes," Remy gasped. "Yes, of course. God, you, you *dunderheed*." He sniffed. "Fuck. We're doing this."

"Yes," Ash whispered fervently, elatedly.

"Good. Because this past week has really sucked."

"Aye. It has. Been utter shite."

"Well, it's looking up." Remy gave a watery smile.

Ash took a deep shuddering breath and pressed their foreheads together. "Aye."

"Good." Remy kissed him, then pulled back with an hysterical choked laugh. "I'm gonna have to email that professor again. Tell him no thanks after all."

"*Mythfits* will keep you." Ash squeezed him. "And you'll just have to publish that novel."

"Yeah. Guess so," Remy agreed, and Ash cupped his cheek and gave him another lingering kiss. He couldn't help it.

"How about we have dinner," Ash murmured.

"Dinner is good." They turned to the room service cart, and Ash noticed the two plates for the first time. He snorted. "You and Etta planned this?"

Remy smiled. "She might have given me your room number."

"I'd complain about meddling, but I cannae gripe about what brings me you." He shuffled closer again.

"Aw, you romantic, you." Remy smiled and ran a finger down the tip of Ash's nose. "We owe her, it's true."

Ash hummed and kissed Remy again, just because he could.

His stomach growled.

Remy pulled back with a laugh. "Come on, my dunderheid, show me what you cooked me for dinner." He laced their fingers together and took a step toward the room service trolley.

Ash murmured, "With pleasure," and helplessly followed Remy to the food.

# *Epilogue*

**"HAMISH** and Niall are my favorites," gushed the young fan who'd introduced himself with a breathy "I'm Steph." Below his impressive afro, he gave Ash a wide-eyed look that could only be described as worshipful.

Ash gave him a genuine smile. "Thank you." He leaned forward conspiratorially. "They're mine too. Niamish forever, right?"

The kid about swooned and floated away clutching his picture to his skinny chest.

"I think he might be in love," Remy whispered, as incorrigible a con partner as Etta.

Ash looked over and wrinkled his nose. Remy winked.

He was sat to Ash's left and a little behind, with his phone in hand, a front-row seat to the autograph session, his favorite part of any con. He loved watching the fans get excited over Ash and heap praise on him, he said. He also loved the easy access it gave him to all the cosplays—he took the picture of anyone who came to Ash's table dressed in costume. Having your picture taken by #AshsBoyfriend tended to be the goal of his fans now. Ash fucking loved it.

An hour later, the last fan in the queue—which had been cut off for the day—shyly approached with her arms wrapped tightly round a sketchbook.

She pointed to a picture of Ash as Zvi and gave a tiny smile when Ash read her name off the Post-it and introduced himself. "Pleasure to meet you, Alice." He signed the photo with one of Zvi's lines—"I'm a man AND a wolf."—and scrawled his name. "Are you having a good weekend?" he asked, hoping she'd open up a bit. He never wanted his shier fans to feel they'd wasted an opportunity.

"Oh yes," she breathed.

Ash smiled encouragingly. "That's good."

"I have something for you," she blurted. She flushed bright red but fumbled with her sketchbook and pulled out—

"Holy shit," Remy breathed.

Holy shit indeed. She'd sketched Hamish in his brownie form, using regular pencil for him, but colored pencils to accent his fairy features and markings and to surround him with blooming flowers and artistic magicky-looking swirls. It was stunning.

"Wow. That's beautiful." He gladly accepted it when she pushed it closer. "Thank you, Alice. You're very talented."

Remy nodded enthusiastically. "That is so getting framed and put up on the wall."

A year ago, several months after Remy had started going to cons as Ash's plus-one and after he'd moved into Ash and Etta's place, Remy had co-opted one of the walls in the main room for "The Shrine."

On it Remy hung all of his favorite pieces of fanart Ash had been given. It was filling up fast, though, and they'd have to start rotating soon.

Alice turned even pinker and squeaked, "Thank you." Then she dug into her sketchbook and pulled out something else. "I heard you write all the werewolf stories, so I...." Looking even more nervous than she had with the first one, she handed Remy another drawing. This one was of Ash and Remy holding one of the many malamute puppies *Mythfits* had guest starred over the three series.

"Whoa," Remy breathed.

"I saw you yesterday at the tables. I hope you don't mind—" Alice started, but Remy jumped out of his seat and wrapped her in a bear hug.

"Alice, you made my day. Thank you so much!" Remy pulled back so he could grin at her and at the sketch, his gaze bouncing between the two. "No one has ever made me anything before. This is so fucking awesome. Thank you."

Ash nodded. "Definitely, thank you." On impulse, he grabbed another shot—as Hamish this time—and quickly wrote—*To a fabulous artist—thank you!* Then he stacked it with the one she'd paid for and handed them both over.

"Oh, you don't—" she protested, but Ash shook his head.

"It's the least I can do. Anyone who makes him smile like that deserves so much more." He nodded his head to the still-beaming Remy.

"It was my pleasure," Alice whispered and hurried away.

"Ash, Aaaash, looook." Remy held out his drawing. "She made me *art*."

"I saw that," Ash said as he stood and guided Remy out of the hall with a hand on the small of his back. Remy practically skipped all the way.

"This is so cool."

"Another for 'The Shrine'?"

"I can hear the air quotes when you say it like that," Remy muttered, but not with anger. "And of course not, this one is too special. Maybe the office?"

About a week after he moved in, Remy took over Ash's unused office so he could work on "the next great Canadian novel—or you know, some werewolf fantasy romp that sells a few copies."

"I think," Ash said as they reached the exit, "your office is the perfect place to hang your first piece of art, sweetheart." Then he leaned forward and kissed Remy sweetly on the mouth for all the con to see.

# *Coming in June 2019*

REAMSPUN DESIRES

**Dreamspun Desires #83**
**The More the Merrier** by Sean Michael

Too much of a good thing?

When Logan gets the call about newborn triplets in need of a home, he steps up, realizing too late the daunting task he's taken on. He'd be lost without the men of the Teddy Bear Club—especially Dirk.

Dirk even offers to spend spring break at Logan's home, helping him and the babies settle in. He loves being a dad, and he wants to help Logan find the same joy. It doesn't hurt that they enjoy spending time together.

Before they even realize it, they're settling into a routine… becoming a family.

Falling in love.

But their new bond is about to face the ultimate test. Will they come through and realize that with love, there's no such thing as enough?

**Dreamspun Desires #84**
**Fake Dating the Prince** by Ashlyn Kane

A royal deception. An accidental romance.

When fast-living flight attendant Brayden Wood agrees to accompany a first-class passenger to a swanky charity ball, he discovers his date—"Call me Flip"—is actually His Royal Highness Prince Antoine-Philipe. And he wants Brayden to pretend to be his boyfriend.

Being Europe's only prince of Indian descent—and its only gay one—has led Flip to select "appropriate" men first and worry about attraction later. Still, flirty, irreverent Brayden captivates him right away, and Flip needs a date to survive the ball without being match-made.

Before Flip can pursue Brayden in earnest, the paparazzi forces his hand, and the charade is extended for the remainder of Brayden's vacation.

Posh, gorgeous, thoughtful Prince Flip is way out of Brayden's league. If Brayden survives three weeks of platonically sharing a bed with him during the romantic holiday season, going home afterward might break his heart.…